Hurricane Mia

a Caribbean Adventure

Donna Marie Seim

Donna Marie Seim

Peapod Press
2010

Peapod Press, an imprint of PublishingWorks, Inc.
151 Epping Road
Exeter, NH 03833
603-778-9883

For Sales and Orders:
603-772-7200

Designed by: Melodica Design
Cover designed by: Sarah Raleigh of Raleigh Designs

LCCN: 2010925874
ISBN-13: 978-0-9826911-0-6

Printed on recycled paper.

Printed by McNaughton & Gunn

This book is a work of fiction. Any resemblance to persons living or deceased is completely coincidental.

Hurricane Mia

a Caribbean Adventure

Acknowledgments

I would like to extend my tremendous appreciation for all the very special people who supported my writing of *Hurricane Mia*. Without them I would have been lost at sea!

From the beginning I would like to thank Pegi Deitz Shea, who supported my initial idea of *Hurricane Mia* and helped steer me through the first six chapters. I would like to thank Mark Karlins for his continued support of my writing, and of *Hurricane Mia* in particular. I would like to thank Bryan Naqqi Manco for taking me on the eco tour of a lifetime and introducing me to the wonderful people and Bush Medicine of Middle Caicos. I would like to thank Kaylan Adair, who gave me the hardest task of all, to rewrite, revise, and redirect *Hurricane Mia*! I would like to thank my friend and mentor Troon Adams Harrison for her ultimate wisdom, for keeping me on track, and for always being kind, even when her critiques were not what I wanted to hear. I would like to thank Jeremy Townsend, and a big thanks to all the great folks at Peapod Press, for believing in *Hurricane Mia* and helping me polish her to a nice bright sheen, reader ready!

I would like to thank Skye Wentworth, my publicist, for every single brilliant idea she has come up with! And, most importantly, I want to thank Susan Spellman for her breathtaking illustrations and for continually reading my mind and making my characters come to life!

None of this would ever have been possible without the love and of support of my husband, Martin, who is, at times, a saint. And my daughter, Kristin, who is responsible for encouraging me to write down my stories and who is always there for me!

AN UNWANTED SUMMER
Chapter 1

Mia stepped out of the airplane onto the ladder. The humid tropical air engulfed her with such smothering force she gasped. The glare of the midday sun made her squint. She felt her hair curling into tight ringlets and drops of perspiration forming on the tip of her nose. The propellers of the small puddle-jumper deafened her. She clung to the railing, feeling her way down the ladder like an old lady.

She still couldn't believe that she was wasting her entire summer vacation with her grandparents. It was unfair. She and her best friend Sam had discussed every detail of their trip to a camp in Maine for months. Mia had tingled with anticipation as Sam described the huge stables filled with horses. She said the lake was so clear and clean you could see your toes. And Sam's dad had just bought a motorboat for towing their new wave boards. Mia had spent all her waking hours daydreaming about it. She had crossed off the months, weeks, and days on her calendar till summer came.

Now her world was upside down. It all changed the day Mia's mom told her she was sick. She had never been given a choice. The plane tickets for her and her brother were bought before she even knew about it. Mia bristled with resentment.

She'd been to Gram and Gramp's island in the Caribbean before. It was hot and sticky there, especially in the summer, and there was absolutely *nothing* to do. And Jack, her snaggle-toothed little brother, was no prize. He could drive her crazy in a minute or less. And if all of that wasn't bad enough, there was Gram to deal with.

Last spring was still fresh in her memory, when her parents went to Europe and her grandparents came to stay with her and Jack. It was the longest month of her life. Gram made rules about everything! No shoes on in the house! No friends sleeping over! No TV on school nights! No food in the living room! No sleeping in on Saturday! No instant messaging until chores were done! And on and on the rules marched until she became dizzy... Mia could never understand how her father could be so fun loving while his mother was so darn mean!

Mia snapped to attention when she heard a hearty greeting boom above the airport commotion. "Mia! Jack! Welcome to Bambarra!"

There stood Gramps, tall and smiling, his arms extended for a big bear hug. Gram looked severe with her white hair pulled straight back from her tanned face, all tied up in a turquoise scarf. Mia, even seeing Gramps, could not forget for a moment how she dreaded being on this remote island for an entire summer. She knew she would be bored to tears!

Gramps' hug felt warm and welcoming, but Mia stiffened when Gram's face radiated immediate disapproval. "Mia! I cannot believe you are wearing torn blue jeans for your travel clothes on the plane!"

"It wasn't one plane! It was three planes, and we had to get dressed in the middle of the night to make the first flight out of Boston. I wanted to wear my pajamas, but Mom wouldn't let me." Mia could feel her temper rising. Who in the world cared, besides Gram, what she wore on the stupid plane?

Gramps grabbed their suitcases and led them out to the parking lot. Mia and Jack scrambled into the back of the old pickup truck, perching themselves on the wooden bench behind the window. Gramps hoisted their suitcases and backpacks into the bed of the truck. He climbed into the cab, next to Gram, revved the motor, and threw the truck into gear, pulling out onto the sandy stone road. Mia felt the hot air swirl around her. Each time the truck hit a pothole, she and Jack bounced up in the air and were forced to grab onto the wooden bench beneath them. Mia coughed as white dust billowed out from behind the truck as it rambled down the road.

Small herds of donkeys peppered the roadside. A baby donkey sidled up to its mother, blinking at Mia and Jack as the truck whisked by. Wild horses were gathered in groups of three or four. They were smaller than regular horses, with coats of amber brown. Each had a white star on its forehead and several had one "white sock." They swished their tails as they nibbled stubby chunks of weed grass. They made Mia think about the horse at camp named Christmas, a handsome Tennessee Walker. Sam had shown her his picture and promised Mia that she could ride him first. Gram pointed out some of the historic sights as they drove by, but Mia was not listening. All she could think about was her ruined summer.

The truck rounded a corner, giving them a wide-angle view of the ocean. Jack yelped, "Wahoo! Thar' she blows!" The water, to Mia, looked angry, moving and churning, sending one wave after another crashing onto the sandy shore.

Heedless of the drama of the sea, the truck rolled on, passing a sleepy outdoor café surrounded by limestone walls. A girl, sitting on the wall, caught Mia's eye as they passed by. She was surrounded by blooming bougainvillea in brilliant hues of red and pink, cascading over a gated stonewall that led into the café's garden.

Mia spotted a white-feathered bird standing on top of a whitewashed wall. He stood four feet tall on black stilt-like legs. His beak, a brilliant orange-gold, seemed large for his small head and skinny neck. He stood stone still, watching her as they drove by. Mia sighed, wondering if he felt as alone as she did.

Gramps pulled over to the curb and parked the truck. "Time to get the mail!" He walked through a cobble-stoned courtyard, past two shiny black cannons.

"Must be cannons from an old shipwreck!" Jack said as he hopped out of the truck. Mia decided to jump out and stretch her cramped legs. Gramps retrieved his mail quickly from a locked box. Walking back to the truck, he waved at a couple of resting men. In return, they nodded their heads and touched the wide brims of their straw hats.

"Good Afta'noon. What brings you out here in de midday sun?" asked the one with the biggest smile.

"Just been to the airport to pick up my two grandkids from Boston," Gramps said, gesturing toward Mia and Jack.

"Oh, dat be fine! Your grands dey reach Bambarra safe, now dat be jus' fine," the friendly man said, clicking his tongue.

Jack had his new digital camera and was snapping pictures like crazy. Mia felt burdened by him. With his thick glasses, scarecrow straight hair, and toothy grin, Jack often ended up

4

as the center of attention— negative attention. The kids at school picked on him because he was small for his age, and, at ten years old, way too smart for his own good. Mia knew that short and smart don't make for a lot of friends. She and Jack were total opposites.

Mia's attention was diverted by the sight of a man riding a horse down the middle of the street. She watched as the man rode up to her. The horse didn't have a saddle, only a striped woolen rug thrown over its back. The man seemed too large for the horse, his bare feet dangling far below its belly. He used an old rope as reins. The man smiled widely, showing off a golden tooth. His hair stuck out in wild tufts, tamed partially by clusters of short braids. He wore patched denim jeans and a loose fitting poncho tie-dyed the colors of the rainbow. The bright colors glowed against his brown skin.

He waved his hand in the air. "My bee-u-tiful lady! You want to take a ride? She be very genteel."

"I'd love to pat him."

The man waved his hand invitingly toward the horse.

Mia stretched her fingers out and felt the fuzzy warm muzzle. The horse didn't pull away from her, but leaned forward into her strokes.

"Velvet! He feels like velvet! What's his name?"

"Her name be Sawndee!" The man threw one leg over the horse and slid the short distance to the ground. He bent over and made a stirrup out of his two hands. Mia slipped her foot into his hands and felt herself lifted up in the air. In a split second she was seated on the horse's back. She breathed in its sweet smell. The rope was soft and supple in her hands.

"Mia! Get off of that horse! Good gracious! What are you doing?" Gram yelled out the window of the truck.

"Oops, sorry. I guess I gotta go, but thanks anyway!" Mia's cheeks flushed as she hurriedly dismounted. She was embarrassed by her grandmother's rudeness.

Unruffled, the man hopped back on his horse and clicked his tongue. "My lady ride her on island, maybe sometime!" Sandy broke into a lively trot, her hooves clopping against the hard cobblestone road as she disappeared from Mia's view.

"C'mon Mia, get in before we leave without you!" Jack called. Mia reluctantly climbed back into the truck. Being left behind didn't sound so awful to her.

They rattled onward through the town, passing a bright pink library, a white stucco church with red doors, and a glass-fronted bank. A flock of chickens dashed out of an alleyway, followed by a rooster. Gramps didn't even tap the brakes of the truck. The chickens squawked as they ran into a cracked hole in a nearby wall, and the rooster glared at the truck as if it had no right to rile his ladies.

Jack continued to fiddle with his digital camera. It was his birthday present from Mom and Dad. It irritated Mia, though she had no reason to be jealous. Her present from them was exactly what she had wished for: a new wave-board. But she had left it leaning against the wall in her bedroom, unused. She had no desire to use it in Bambarra, not without Sam, and not in salty, shark-infested waters.

The truck took a sharp left. Mia and Jack swayed sideways, grabbing on to each other. Gramps called, "Crabtree Corner coming up. We'll be home soon."

Crabtree Corner was filled with sleeping dogs. Three in a row snoozed in the shade of an abandoned car. One pup with springy ears was busy digging a good-sized hole. It made Mia feel homesick. Rags, her dog, dug holes too.

The houses in Crabtree were painted bright shades of yellow, blue, and green. One had handmade brooms propped outside the open door. Mia watched as two little boys sat on the doorstep poking each other in the belly and laughing. A woman in a long printed housedress stuck her head out the door and waved as the truck rolled by.

Gramps veered to the right and headed up a winding road that climbed higher and higher. The sun shone so strong it created a mirage of wavering lines on the powdery road. The truck lurched as Gramps hit the brakes in front of the familiar painted green gate.

"Hop out, gate boy. Undo the latch and swing her open," Gramps yelled out the window. Jack hopped to it, allowing the truck to pass through. Mia felt trapped as she watched Jack close the gate behind them. She shuddered as she heard the click of the latch.

SEA SNAILS AND CELL PHONES
Chapter 2

The house was nestled into the side of the ridge. From the garage, Mia saw the solid expanse of ocean interrupted only by the little island of Turtle Cay. The colors ranged from the darkest shades of indigo to vibrant hues of turquoise and green. Gramps pointed to the East. "Do you see the white caps rolling way out by the darkest waters? It's a heavy sea today! Those are powerful waves crashing into the reef."

"Hey look, there is Turtle Cay!" Mia remembered the little island and how she thought it looked so lonely out in the sea by itself.

"It's pronounced key," Gram corrected her. "Our little islands are called keys." Mia sucked her breath in. Who cares if they are called keys or cays, an island is an island!

Gramps unloaded the suitcases from the truck. Everyone grabbed one, and formed a small parade walking the narrow pathway to the house. They entered through a courtyard, enclosed on three sides, that was painted a dark soothing green. Despite herself, Mia liked the room; it was cool, both in temperature and on her eyes, and it had a hammock in it.

"Welcome to our island home!" Gramps smiled. "We're so happy you could share your summer with your old grandparents!"

Gram looked down at Mia's feet and said, "Don't forget to take your outside shoes off before we go inside."

Gram opened a door from the courtyard that led into a hallway with three doors. She pointed to the first door and let Mia walk in. "Mia, this one is yours. It's the small one, but I hope you will be comfortable. Jack, you get your dad's old room down the hall."

Mia's room was painted a bright yellow. The bed was pushed tight against the wall, covered by a blue and lavender patchwork quilt. Just past the foot of the bed, a white lace curtain, framing a window, billowed and danced in the sea breeze. A rattan dresser stood against the wall. Above the dresser was a photo of Mia's mom and dad; they were much younger and had swimsuits on. Her mom's hair was blonde and curly just like hers. Mia stared at the picture, feeling a lump growing in her throat.

The only other piece of furniture in the room was a wooden desk. Standing alone on the desk was a glass bottle filled with a bouquet of pink periwinkles. Mia sighed; She dug deep into her backpack and pulled out the red nail polish her mom had given her. Next to that she lined up her travel jewelry box, her colored pencils and notebook, a can of baby powder, and her non-allergenic skin lotion. Not satisfied, she plunked down her iPod, cell phone, and charger. It still didn't feel right, so Mia set to unpacking all her things, giving the room a cozy, cluttered feeling. The last thing she pulled out of her bag was the big scruffy stuffed dog Sam had given her for her birthday, the day she turned twelve. She was happy that day. She had named the dog Rags after her real dog.

She could hear Jack exclaiming down the hallway. "Cool! This is a wicked awesome room!"

Why did his voice have to penetrate through everything? She put her hands over her ears, trying to block it out. She threw herself on the bed squeezing her stuffed dog tight. The air seemed heavy and more humid than Mia was used to. She felt woozy; the room spun around, forcing her to sit up. She placed one foot on the ground to steady her nerves.

She needed to talk to Sam! Mia reached for her cell phone, snapped it open, and clicked Sam's name. She waited. Nothing. She looked at the screen: *call failed*. She tried again and again. It was no use. She was cut off from the rest of the world, her world! She felt dizzy . . . her chest was tight. She buried her face into her stuffed dog, but it didn't smell like the real one. She felt she would surely die forced to spend an entire summer without Sam! Mia shook the stuffed dog and spoke to him, "If Sam were here she would make me laugh and Rags would lick my face and wag his tail! You are just a dumb stuffed dog!"

Jack barged into her room wearing his swimming trunks. "Ya wanna go down to the beach?"

"No, dope! Get out of my room! Can't you leave me alone for one minute?"

"Stay in your stupid room, I don't care!" He was gone before she could reply.

She opened the rattan dresser and pulled out a pair of denim shorts and her favorite t-shirt that said "BOSTON IS THE BEST." She slipped on a well-worn pair of flip-flops and found her way to the bathroom. She ran the cold water as hard as it could go, but it stayed lukewarm. She splashed it over her face and arms. On her way out, she caught sight of a note taped to the wall between the toilet and the sink.

Washing up: Turn water on, wet hands, turn faucet off immediately!
Soap up, then rinse quickly!
Please do the same for showers and washing hair.
Toilet flushing! If it is yellow, let it mellow.
If it is brown, flush it down.
Remember every drop of our island water is precious!

"Ewww!" Mia groaned out loud. Gram and her never-ending rules!

She whistled through her teeth. This was going to be one long, hot summer. She peeked around the corner and tiptoed into the coolness of the courtyard. There were huge terracotta pots with purple and red blossoms tumbling down their curved sides. The air smelled spicy like vanilla and sweet jasmine. A mint green lizard lounged on a piece of driftwood, partially camouflaged by the dappled shade. Mia studied him as close as she dared. To her surprise, he turned in her direction and winked at her, as he did one quick push-up. "Hey little fella! You're in great shape. I bet you're ready to run the Boston Marathon!"

Mia went in from the courtyard through the kitchen door and announced to Gram, "I unpacked."

"That's good, dear." Gram held a large wooden mallet.

"What's the hammer for?" Mia asked.

"I'm preparing a Caribbean dinner for us. The conch needs to be pounded and then marinated in lime juice for the best taste." Gram pointed to a pile of slimy sea snails. Mia's stomach lurched.

"Don't worry, I'm also making baked paw paws. Gramps loves them. I stuff them with tomatoes, beef, and cheese. But the real secret is in the spices."

Mia grimaced. Man, she could really go for a cheeseburger and fries.

"I need to call my friend Sam. My cell phone won't work here."

"Well, Mia, if you call the States from here it's very expensive. Why don't you wait until later in the visit, when you have more to talk about?"

Mia tried not to let her impatience show. "Sam is taking care of Rags for me and they're leaving tomorrow for a vacation in Maine."

"Oh, Rags is going with them?"

"Yes, Rags is going with them because I'm not there to take care of him! Mom made me come here because she didn't want Jack to come alone. He doesn't need me. He's not a baby! Besides, Sam had asked me to go on vacation with her ages ago and both Mom and Dad had said yes. But that was before Mom got sick." Mia took a deep breath.

"I'm sorry to hear that, Mia, I didn't know you were so unhappy about coming to visit us." Gram's voice sounded strained. "But this is where your mother wanted you and Jack to be."

Mia felt her cheeks flush hot. "Gram, I really do need to call Sam. Please! I'll pay you back for the phone call."

"Go ahead, Mia, it seems like you'll be miserable if you don't. Just don't stay on too long."

Gram showed her the phone and Mia dialed the number hungrily. She listened for the ring but it made no sound at all. Mia scrunched up her nose and tried again. "Gram, there isn't a dial tone. The phone isn't working."

"Oh dear, the phone must be out. That happens all the time on the island. It'll come back soon, maybe by tomorrow."

"Tomorrow they'll be gone! And what about Mom and Dad? How can we call them without a phone?" She felt her temper rising.

Mia stomped out of the kitchen onto the veranda. She tried to calm herself but she couldn't, it was just too much! It was her mom's fault. Why did she have to get sick? Mia tried to push it out of her mind. She didn't want to remember how her mom started to slow down, the mom that could do everything. She got thinner and her eyes didn't have that sparkle anymore, the way they used to. Mia hated that awful day that she came home from school to find her mother in bed. Her mom's hair lay thin and limp on the pillow, and when she opened her eyes they looked tired and strained. She whispered to Mia that she must be strong for her. Mia didn't want to be strong for her mom or herself or anybody else, including her brother, Jack. All she wanted was for life to be the way it was before, before her mom got sick.

Sea Snails and Cell Phones

Mia's eyes stung. The reflection was strong from the water below. She raised her hand to shade her eyes. Two figures were in the water, diving into the waves and riding on them like surfboards. Gramps rode his wave all the way to the shore. Jack looked like a playful otter chasing one wave after the other. Mia felt miserable, left out, and alone.

A GREEN FLASH
Chapter 3

The next morning the phone rang and Mia sprinted from the breakfast table to answer it. Jack was on her heels, but Mia reached the phone first.

"Hello, this is the Petersons' residence."

"Hi Mia, it's Mom."

"Hi, Mom, finally it's you! How's Rags? Did Sam come and get him okay?"

"Yes, Rags got off just fine. Samantha will take good care of him."

"Did you give Sam all Ragsie's stuff? Did you remember Squirrelly, his toy?"

"Yes, Sam and her dad took all his things, including the leash and brush that you forgot to pack."

"Well, we were in a rush!"

"How are you and Gram getting along?"

"Okay, I guess. But, Mom, it's really *boring* here! And my cell phone doesn't work. Dad *promised* me it would and it doesn't!"

Jack was breathing down her neck bending his ear to the phone receiver. Mia wanted to smack him.

17

"Don't worry about your cell phone, just enjoy your summer and remember that I love you."

"I love you, Mom!" A wave of homesickness washed over her as she handed the phone to Jack. "Here, but be quick about it, I need to call Sam!"

Mia dialed Sam's number over and over leaving desperate messages for her to call her back. Gram caught her red handed, in the middle of a message. "No more phone calls! It's expensive to call the States. I'm sorry but that is the way it is here!"

Mia hid in the hammock. She couldn't stand to look at her grandmother.

One whole week had passed since their arrival. Nothing exciting ever happened up on the ridge and time dragged by. Mia lounged on the hammock and read five of the paperback books she had brought along. Gramps and Jack took trips to town in the truck when they weren't working on one project or another. Gramps spent way too much time with Jack, and Mia resented that, but at least it kept Jack out of her hair most of the time.

Mia needed to escape, away from the house and her brother. She peeked in the garage. Jack was busy working on building a ship model with Gramps. Gram was nowhere to be seen. This was her chance. She grabbed her bag, packed her iPod, and slipped out the kitchen door. Mia quickened her pace as she approached the gate. She unlatched it in one motion, but was met with resistance when she tried to swing it open. It was more difficult than it looked when Jack did it. The gate was heavy and it scraped against the road as she hauled it to one side. The sun was burning down and she could feel her hair starting to frizz in the humidity. Gram had yammered on and on about how the gate always needed to be closed, but it was too heavy, and besides, she wouldn't be gone long. She'd just close it up tight when she got back.

Mia reached Crabtree Corner. The dogs she had seen when they first drove by were there, sleeping wherever they could find a spot of shade. The doors to all of the houses were closed tight, even the one with the brooms outside that looked like a store. She walked on past the Salinas. Gramps had told her all about how they made salt from the sea in the Salinas, how they raked it until the water evaporated and the salt crystals were formed. Now, it was a great fishing hole for tons of birds, like long-legged herons and brown pelicans. She wasn't sure which side road led to town, so she chose the first one she came to. It was more of an alleyway than a road. A car passed close by and the driver gave her a wave as if they were old friends. Mia ignored him.

At the end of the road, she heard waves crashing into the break-wall that ran along the ocean side of Front Street. As she rounded the corner, the sea mist settled on her face. On the other side of the street stood a whitewashed limestone wall that ran the length of the road, interrupted now and then by a gate.

There, sitting on the wall, was a girl, the girl she had seen from the back of the truck. She was sitting under the shade of an enormous bougainvillea tree. She tilted her head to one side as Mia approached. She did not speak. Mia walked on by, preferring not to acknowledge her.

"Hey girl, you lost?"

Mia, curious, spun around. "No, I'm not lost. Just don't know where I'm going."

"You visitin' the island?" The girl smiled at Mia.

"Yes. Do you live here? I mean, do you live here on Bambarra?"

The girl answered her with a nod of her head, and then pointed to the house that was half hidden behind the wall. There dangling from the porch was a hand-painted sign. Mia read it out loud, "THE GREEN FLASH CAFÉ." Beneath it in smaller letters it read, "*cold drinks, good eats.*"

"Is that your café?" Mia asked.

"Yes, it's my mama's café."

"Is it open? Can I get a cold soda?"

She nodded her head, "Yes, that'd be fine."

"What's your name?"

"Neisha. What yours be?"

"Mia."

Neisha hopped down from her perch and slid behind the wall. She opened the gate and gestured for Mia to enter. Then she closed the gate and latched it tight.

"Why don't you leave the gate open? Don't you want people to come in?" Mia asked.

"Donkeys! They eat everythin'. Mama hollas up a storm if I be leavin' it open."

Mia wondered if she should have closed her grandparents' gate. But what donkey would dare to come into her Gram's yard?

Mia followed Neisha into the dark café. She welcomed the prickly feeling of goose bumps as the coolness rushed to greet her. She wiped the sweat from her forehead and the tip of her nose with her t-shirt. There were tables, different shapes and colors, scattered around the room. In the far back was a bar, a simple structure made of bamboo poles laced together with rope. Hanging over the bar was an awning made of woven palm leaves. It gave the whole room a tropical feeling. Mia breathed in. The room smelled good, like spicy French fries. Behind the counter was a woman with a starched white apron tied around her middle. She was a big woman, especially compared to Neisha. She welcomed Mia with a warm smile.

"Neisha, who's dat you found out dere in the midday sun? You is lucky you hain't been roasted alive. Neisha, go get this chile a cold cola from da coola."

Neisha pulled out two cans and slapped them down on the nearest table. She expertly popped both tabs and handed one already sweaty can to Mia. Mia gratefully took it and poured half the can down her throat. It was deliciously cool and peppery. As Mia placed the can back on the table, a bois-terous burp exploded from deep inside her. It echoed in the empty café. Neisha put her hand over her mouth, trying to stifle a giggle. Mia let out a snort-hiccup ending with a high-pitched squeak. "Oh my gosh, I sound like a pig!" The two girls surrendered themselves to contagious giggles.

"No more, Neisha! Please stop! Really, it hurts," Mia cried. Neisha's mama was laughing too, and shaking her head from side to side.

"You sure be silly, girls. Yes sir, you sure be silly."

Mia ended up spending the entire afternoon in the café. Neisha showed her how to refill the mustard and ketchup containers. They stacked the white paper napkins in the metal dispensers on each table and topped up the salt and pepper-shakers. Mia learned about putting uncooked rice in the salt to keep it from sticking in the humidity. They took turns sweep-ing the floor with an old worn broom. Mia watched as Neisha waited tables and brought drinks and short order meals of fried fish and conch to the customers. There weren't many, only a couple of fishermen and a pair of deep-sea divers.

"Why aren't there more customers?" Mia asked.

"It be Sunday, so most folks be goin' to church two times. They go for the morning service and again for the night ser-vice. They be staying home in the afta'noon. Not many away folk be comin' in the summa' time." Neisha explained.

"Do you go to church twice?" Mia found this incredible.

"Na, mama and I go in the mornin'. We got to keep the café open in the afta'noon and evening."

Mia looked at her watch. "I gotta go!" she said, suddenly panicky. "It's way later than I thought. Gram will kill me."

"Can you come back tomorrow?"

"Maybe, but it isn't easy getting out of prison!"

"What you talkin' about prison?" Neisha looked concerned.

"That's a joke, never mind, I'll try."

"I be sittin' on the wall, waitin'." Neisha smiled.

"Thanks for the soda, Mrs... umm," Mia stammered.

"You welcome, honey. You can jus' call me Bianca." Her face lit up with a smile.

The sun sent long shadows on the Salinas as Mia retraced her route back to the ridge. She felt light at heart for the first time in a long time. It wasn't anywhere near the same as having her best friend Sam, but Neisha seemed nice and the café was really cool. Maybe her summer wouldn't be so horrid after all.

BLAME DONKEY
Chapter 4

Mia approached the opened gate. What was happening? There were shouts, whoops, and wild screams, interspersed with blood curdling heeeee's and haaaaaw's! Mia charged down the driveway. Her knees felt like rubber, her feet barely touched the ground. She stopped dead in her tracks as a donkey came skidding out of the courtyard. It was followed by Gram wielding a broom and smacking it on its hind end. "Out, out! You dirty animal! Get out!!"

Mia jumped out of the way of the panic-stricken donkey. Gram charged by Mia, her face red with rage. Her hair, which hung loose, was whipped by the wind in all directions. "What's happening?" Mia called after her.

"Donkeys! In the courtyard! They are eating all of my flowers!"

Mia dashed down the winding driveway to find the catastrophe that awaited her. The donkeys were everywhere! Feasting in the gardens and down the lane to the beach. Gramps and Jack were busy at the bottom end trying to round up the donkeys with a rope and lasso. Mia grabbed a mop and went after a mother and baby that had settled in

"Out, out! You dirty animal! Get out!!"

the courtyard. She swung out the mop hollering, "You dumb donkeys! Get out!"

The mother donkey, protective of her baby, kicked her hind legs at Mia, knocking over a terra cotta pot. The earthenware exploded in a thousand pieces as it hit the hard tile floor. The braying that came out of that animal made Mia's blood curdle. The baby donkey wedged itself between its mother and the kitchen door. In a fearful frenzy, it kicked its hooves, making dents in the doorframe and ripping the screens to shreds. Mia, refusing to give up, charged the mother again, waving the mop and shouting, "Get out! Get out and take your baby with you!" But Mia made sure to keep her distance from the mother donkey. She didn't want to come in contact with a donkey hoof!

Gram returned to the scene with her flailing broom, and smacked the baby donkey on its rump. The baby, terrified, leaped out from behind the door and skidded into the middle of the courtyard. Mia wielded her mop at the mother donkey, managing to knock down a hanging planter. It crashed to the floor, spooking the baby donkey, whom then proceeded to pee all over the floor. Mia was hopping over dirt and donkey droppings as she tried once more to get the mother out of the courtyard. With both Mia and Gram wielding brooms and mops, the mother donkey took flight with her baby at her tail. Mia, with her mop, ushered them up the drive toward the gate, then gasped in utter frustration: the gate was closed tight. How was she supposed to get two donkeys out without letting the one on the other side back in? Gram came charging back up the driveway like a soldier without its horse, broom poised high in the air ready to strike. She opened the gate, threatening the donkey on the outside with her broom while Mia and her mop worked the other two forward and out the gate. Bam! Gram slammed the gate shut and latched it tight.

In the distance, Mia could hear Jack whooping in his attempts to lasso a donkey. She watched as he encircled the rope around its neck. Jack proudly walked it on the lead of the rope, as if it were tame, toward Mia and the gate. Gramps rounded up the last of the stray donkeys. He ushered them toward the lower gate that led down to the beach. Mia ran to help Gramps. Jack, having released his captured donkey, quickly caught up. He had the rope wound over his shoulder like a cowboy. Mia felt silly carrying a mop.

By the time they reached the gate, Gramps had all but one cornered. Jack ran after the escapee while Mia hightailed it to the beach gate. Mia sprung the latch and swung the gate open. The donkeys, having had enough of a romp, trotted happily out the gate. Jack, in hot pursuit of the last one, ran around in circles trying to lasso him. Gramps and Mia, running through burr grass and wild bush, came to help. They surrounded the donkey on three sides. He kicked up his hind hooves in protest and voiced a loud and long *heeeee haaaaw*. With his ears flat against his head, he bolted between Mia and Gramps and out the open gate to join his friends. Mia slammed the gate shut. She was exhausted, covered in sweat and dirt, and extremely thirsty. Jack pushed his glasses up the bridge of his nose and with a tooth-filled grin, said, "Hey Mia! Good job leaving the gate open," then kicked up his heels and hee-hawed up the hill.

Blame Donkey

When Mia reached the house, Gram was standing in the courtyard with her pots broken all around her. When Gram saw Mia she hissed at her, "Where have you been?"

"Sorry, Gram, I just wanted to go for a walk and I ended up in town. I met a girl named Neisha. Her mom owns The Green Flash Café."

Gram's face was white with anger. She peered at Mia over the top half of her eyeglasses, her forehead pinched into a mountain range of wrinkles. "Why didn't you close the gate when you left?"

"It was heavy... I was just going for a short walk, then I met Neisha sitting on the wall and we..."

"How could you be so thoughtless? I have told you time and time again how we must keep the gate closed or the animals will get in!"

Mia was working hard to push down her growing sense of frustration. She looked away from her grandmother.

"And why did you leave without telling us? Jack didn't even know you had gone. If Gramps and I weren't woken up from our siesta by donkeys braying right outside our bedroom window who knows how much more damage they would have done!"

"I just wanted to go for a walk by myself!"

"Well, here's the broom and you have the mop, now you can clean up this mess. What you can't sweep away, you'll need to mop up with water. I have a pail of leftover dish water in the kitchen."

Gram retreated into the kitchen through the battered door. Gramps came around the corner, glanced in Mia's direction, and with a tired voice said, "Well Mia, you know your grandmother's flowers are her prized possessions." Then, shaking his head, he said, "I better fix the kitchen door."

Oh, Mia thought, *I'm never ever going to hear the end of this one!*

She began picking up broken terra cotta pieces and sweeping the potting soil into piles. She found the stench of donkey pee to be quite revolting. Just then Jack showed up.

"Chasing donkeys is wicked fun. I lassoed me a bunch of 'em! Yurggh! What's the stink?" Jack held on to his nose as he investigated.

"Donkey pee mixed with old dishwater!" Mia snapped. "Want some?" She shook the mop at him.

"Whatya' makin', donkey soup? Sure smells like poop. Hee-haw. Mia's the one to blame for the donkey shame. Heehaw." Jack smirked.

"Go away!" Mia felt a laugh growing inside her, but she wasn't going to allow Jack to make her laugh.

"I'm goin', I'm goin'! Gramps is taking me to where he docks his boat. We're gonna take it for a test drive and make sure it's ready for the big trip," Jack said, with his I-know-more-than-you-do look.

"What trip?" Mia spat out the question.

"To Little Turtle Cay." Jack pointed to the only visible island. "We're gonna go tomorrow and have a picnic and feed the stingrays. You're comin' too. Gram said we're all going."

Oh no, Mia thought, *I'm not going on any boat ride tomorrow. I'm going back to The Green Flash Café!*

HUNGRY STINGRAYS
Chapter 5

Mia rammed her iPod into her bag. Why did she have to do what Gram says? Her plans were to meet Neisha at the café, not to go on a silly boat ride. At least they were heading out bright and early. Later on, she would secretly slip into town when Gram and Gramps took their afternoon nap.

Jack had dragged out every piece of snorkeling gear he could find in the garage.

"Hey snorkel boy! How you gonna swim with those flippers on? They look bigger than you!"

"Just you wait, Mia. You're gonna beg me for these flippers when we get there!" Jack put the goggles on, making a fish face at her.

Gram placed cold water bottles in a cooler. "Mia, make sure you have plenty of sunscreen on. The sun is stronger than you realize."

"Yeah, I know, but I want *some* sun to come through. My legs are so white they could blind someone. Fish-belly white is what Sam calls them!" Mia wished that Sam were here with her. When she thought about Sam she thought about Rags and how much she missed him, too, and that made her so sad.

"Make sure that Jack is completely covered with sunscreen," Gram ordered.

"Hey Rudolph, lather yourself up good, and don't forget your nose. " Mia threw the tube of lotion at Jack's head. He caught it and tossed it into his bag of gear.

Gramps and Jack loaded the truck with the cooler, snorkel gear, picnic basket, beach towels, and backpacks. Mia and Jack hopped in the back. As they pulled up to North Creek, Mia spotted a flock of salmon-colored birds wading in the shallows. Flamingoes! Mia had to smile; they looked funny with their legs bending backward at the knee as they stepped gingerly forward, dipping their long, hooked beaks into the water.

On the near side of the creek there were only a handful of boats tied up to individual docks. Some of the boats looked ancient and barely seaworthy, with paint crackling off their hulls. Gramps's boat, the *Dragonfly*, was painted a crisp white with a blue water line; it sat handsomely in the still inlet water of the creek.

Once they were all inside the boat, Gramps began giving boating lessons. "First thing you do is turn on the fan. This is important because the motor needs the air circulation or it could explode from the sudden gas fumes. This is an inboard motor, which means it's inside the boat, like a car."

"Cool, can I turn it on?" Jack asked.

Mia, not being the least bit interested in boating mechanics, put her headphones on and cranked up the volume. Gramps and Jack continued to flip switches and push buttons, and soon they were jetting across the turquoise waters. The creek was pretty, but as they left the inlet and headed out to the open sea, Mia couldn't help herself; she became mesmerized by it. Turtle grass swayed beneath them and colorful fish, all different sizes, darted in and out between the slender blades.

"Do you think we'll see a turtle?" Mia asked, popping her earplugs out.

"You might if you're lucky. They're around, but not always easy to spot." Gramps winked at Mia.

"Didn't you save one once?"

"Yes, I did help a little guy once. He was covered in tar and had just washed up on the shore. He was feeling pretty poorly with all that tar stuck on his shell and flippers. I used my beach towel to wipe him clean as best I could. He didn't try to move; he lay there still as could be. I was worried he was beyond repair."

"But you did save him, right?"

"I carried him into the water and gave him a gentle shove. His flippers went into action and he scrambled back into the turtle grass. I lost sight of him for a while. But later, I spotted him, not more than a few feet away from me. By George, I think he had come back to thank me for lightening his load! Then he took off, heading out toward the reef."

Mia leaned over the side of the boat, straining her eyes, yearning to see a turtle shape in the water. The waves lapped the sides of the boat, and her stomach felt a little queasy. She sat up and plugged her iPod back into her ears. She let the music carry her far away. She closed her eyes, swaying gently with the waves and the music.

Mia opened her eyes in time to see a pelican gliding gracefully in the air. He dove straight down into the water, surfacing with a silvery fish in his beak. A smaller bird came out of nowhere and attacked the pelican from above, trying to steal the fish. What a horrible bird! She was going to ask her grandfather what kind of bird it was when she realized they were approaching Little Turtle Cay. There were no docks in sight, or buildings, or people for that matter, just sand and cliffs.

Gramps brought the boat close to shore, and then with the touch of a button he raised the motor. Without using an anchor, he simply climbed out of the boat and pulled it ashore. Jack hopped off of the back of the boat, not bothering with the ladder. Mia was getting ready to jump in too, when she saw a dark shadow floating close to the back of the boat, exactly where the stairs were. To Mia's great consternation there was another shadow followed by another and another. The boat was being surrounded!

"Ugh! We are being surrounded by stingrays!"

"Yes! They're quite good little beggars," Gram said.

"They want food?" Mia asked.

"They've learned that when boats come, people feed them."

"Wicked! Look at all the stingrays!" Jack yelled from shore.

"Follow me, Mia. Go slow and steady." Gram instructed. "Sudden movement scares them. That's the only time they might sting you. Otherwise, they're as tame as pets."

Gram seemed at ease as she led the way. The stingrays scattered as she entered the water. Mia couldn't take her eyes off them. She didn't want to go in the water, but she didn't want to go alone either, so she slipped into the water close behind Gram.

"Can we feed the stingrays now?" Jack asked as soon as everyone hit the beach.

"Let's give it a go," Gramps said, as he pulled a plastic baggie from the cooler.

"Here's what you do. Take the fish by the tail and hold it out straight." Gramps waded up to just above his knee level. "Put your hand into the water and hold it steady. Tuck your toes in the sand or they might nibble them." A stingray floated gracefully up to Gramps and then retreated. He pulled his hand out of the water and, like a magician, waved to show it was empty. The fish was gone.

"I'm next!" Jack grabbed his fish and headed into the water. A baby-sized ray approached him timidly, swam a loop around him, and took the fish. "Cool! He sucked it right out of my hand!"

Mia wasn't sure she really wanted to feed the stingrays, but she took her fish and entered the water until it was above her knees. She tucked her toes deep into the sand. A stingray floated toward her; it looked like a big black cape. She waited for what seemed like an eternity. Then, suddenly, she felt a sucking current that took the fish out of her fingertips, just like a vacuum cleaner. Her heart was pounding, and she had to admit it was exciting to be feeding a wild sea creature. As Mia started to back out of the water to get another fish, she felt a bump against her leg. A stingray swam behind her. She felt a tickle as the wing brushed her leg. Mia's voice had a touch of panic. "Is he circling me?"

"Stay put, Mia. He won't hurt you if you stay still," Gram answered.

"WOW! Mia, you got a big one!" Jack hollered. "Look! In front of you there's another one. He's a real whopper!"

Mia turned to where Jack was pointing. A black shadow at least four feet across hovered just below the surface of the water.

"Keep calm, Mia." Gramps's voice echoed in her ears. He began to wade toward her.

Mia shivered with fear, and took several large steps backwards, hoping the other ray had glided out of her path. The bottom of her foot hit a hard, sharp object. It sent a piercing pain up her leg. She fell backwards into the water, her knees buckling beneath her.

The giant ray's wing slid over her, blocking out the sun for a split second. Then it was gone. Mia exploded out of the water, arms and legs flailing. Her grandfather was a blur as she bolted past him to safety. "I've been stung!"

"Mia, you weren't stung," Gram said in a matter-of-fact voice.

"My foot hit something sharp. It's bleeding. Maybe it was a stinger." Mia tried to keep her voice from quivering.

"Believe me, you would know it if you were stung. You most likely stepped on the tip of a conch shell. I'll get the emergency kit out of the boat." Gram waded into the ray-filled waters without the slightest hesitation. There had to be at least twenty rays out there!

Mia felt hot tears slide down her face, adding to the mixture of salt and sand. Now she felt stupid. She didn't want to be on this island! She didn't care about feeding stingrays.

What was the point of it all anyway? Why was she being made to do things she didn't really care about?

She and her grandmother were as different as two people could get. Mia had never felt close to her. She felt that her grandmother was always judging her and she was forever coming up short. Mia watched as Gram efficiently fetched the emergency box and waded through the ray-infested water back to shore.

Gram tended Mia's foot. She washed it with some bottled water, then applied a red medicine that stung like crazy. Mia pulled her foot away. "Ouch! That red stuff hurts."

"Hold still, the sting will be over in a minute. You don't want an infected foot, do you?" Gram applied a piece of gauze and wound tape around it to hold it in place. Then she placed Mia's foot on a clean dry towel. "Best you sit still and keep your foot up to stop the bleeding. I think you'll do just fine without stitches or a trip to the doctor." Then she left to help Gramps put out all the lunch preparations.

Jack and Gramps had spread a blanket down and were opening up the cooler. Mia's mouth was so dry her lips stuck together when she tried to talk. "Hey Jack, bring me some cold soda, I am dying of thirst. And, as you can see, I'm an invalid!"

"Here's an orange one, catch!" The soda flew up in the air, just missing Mia. She brushed the sand off of the top, popped it open, and poured it down her throat.

Gram was busy placing colorful plastic dishes and silverware around the blanket. Gramps emptied soda cans into plastic tumblers with little fish painted on them. Grams opened a Tupperware container full of fried chicken legs and placed them with a bowl of chilled pineapple in the middle of the blanket. Next came Gram's spicy German potato salad, honeyed coleslaw and lime drenched conch salad. Lastly, out of a plastic cake box appeared a dark chocolate cake. Jack piled his plate up high, tasting everything. Mia scooted on her bottom, careful to keep her foot in the air, over to the blanket. She looked at all the food on Jack's plate. What a pig he was! He may as well snort! Mia picked at her food; she had felt a little queasy coming over and she didn't want to do anything embarrassing, like throw up, on the way home.

After Jack had completely gorged himself and Gram finished cleaning up from lunch, Gramps announced, "I'm afraid that there are too many stingrays today for snorkeling. And Mia's foot is cut, so we should head on home." Gramps began to gather up their towels.

"I brought all that snorkeling gear for nothin'?" Jack looked totally deflated.

"How about I let you drive the boat on the way home?" Gramps offered.

"I'll be Skipper!" Jack puffed up his chest.

"Yes, you can be the skipper. Mia, I'll carry you back to the boat so your foot doesn't get wet." Gramps scooped Mia up in his strong arms.

Once back on the boat, Mia was relieved to not have any more stingrays to worry about. She watched as Jack pushed buttons and pulled levers to start up the engine. Mia was jealous that Gramps was going to let Jack drive the boat. She was older! She should have been the skipper. But, she had to admit that Jack was smarter about stuff like mechanics. Even so, why did Gramps always pick Jack to do things with, like making models of ships and going to town in the truck? Mia nursed her foot and her hurt feelings.

"Let's drive around the backside of Little Turtle Cay for fun," Gramps suggested. "Yes sir!" Jack answered. Mia watched as the boat circled the island, and another island magically appeared.

"What's that island called?" Jack asked.

"Iguana Cay. And much farther beyond that is Pepper Cay." Gramps added mysteriously, "Iguana Cay is inhabited by a special kind of creature."

"That's easy! Iguanas!" Jack answered.

"Not just any iguana, but a rare species of rock iguana that can be found only in these islands." Gramps raised his bushy white eyebrows. "Wild cats and dogs hunted them almost to extinction. When the Iguana Wildlife Rescue experts learned of this, they had them all moved to this cay where there are no predators."

"How big do they get?" Jack asked.

"They can get big, as much as three feet if allowed to grow to maturity. They're harmless, though. They are strictly vegetarians, eating wild berries mostly."

"Can we go there?" Jack asked.

"That is a trip for another day," Gramps answered.

Mia plugged in her iPod; she didn't want to listen to them any more. It was more important for her to figure out how she was going to sneak back to The Green Flash Café.

THE TEA THAT CURES EVERYTHIN'!
Chapter 6

Mia's foot was still sore from stepping on the conch shell. But that was not going to stop her from going to town to see Neisha. Her grandparents were tired after the boat outing and had settled in for their midday siesta. Jack amused himself with working on the ship model. He had his glasses on and was painting little barrels when Mia peeked in on him.

"Hey, Jack, I'm going to take a walk to town to send some emails. Tell Gram I'll be back before dinner."

"You goin' to that green coffee place? Why can't I come?" Jack whined.

"I'm going by myself, and if you tell Gram I've gone to the Café you are dead meat!"

"Why? I just want to see the place."

"NO! But, if you don't tell, I'll go to the beach with you, I promise."

"But I want to go to the Café!" Jack made a pouting face.

"Act your age! And if you tell, your new digital camera just might disappear in the ocean!" Mia shook her fist at Jack. "I mean it, I will make your life miserable forever!" Then she made her way out the door and up the path to freedom.

Neisha wasn't on her perch on the wall. Mia opened the gate, making sure to shut it tight behind her. She hopped the two steps up to the front porch and peered into the darkened café. Neisha was sitting at the back table folding napkins.

"Hey! Sorry I'm late. My grandparents made me go for a boat ride with my dorky little brother to Little Turtle Cay. It was creepy, have you ever been there?"

"No, I ain't never." Neisha shrugged. "Nobody there anyhow."

"There were tons of stingrays. We fed them little fish. I got a giant one, and it came around behind me and bumped my leg." Mia mimicked the ray hopping on one foot and swooping around Neisha.

"That don't sound like no fun to me," Neisha said, stepping out of her way.

"Well, it was sort of fun to feed them until a huge daddy ray came after me. Then I got spooked, and stepped on a conch shell. I thought I was stung! See my foot?" Mia took off her flip-flop and lifted her foot up, showing off her wound.

"Them rays is used to peoples feedin' them, then they is jus' wantin' more. One lady got stung real bad, she just 'bout died. They's stinger is like being bitten by a poison snake."

"Really? Sure glad I didn't know that when I was out there! Have you ever been to any of the other cays, like Iguana Cay?"

"No." Neisha rolled her eyes.

"Why not? Didn't you tell me that your daddy was a fisherman?"

"Ya, but I be home helping my mama here. I got no need to go chasing them ugly iguanas. Besides, it's not allowed no more. They's protected. Wild cats and dogs used to eat them and folks used to eat them too. They taste just like fried chicken!"

"Neisha! You've eaten one?"

"I be teasin'! I ain't never!" Neisha burst into a contagious giggle.

A small blue-gray bird flew into the open window and landed on the windowsill. The little bird tilted its head to one side, as though inspecting Mia. It twittered noisily. "Chirp, chirp? Chirp, chirp?" Then, as if its questions were answered, it burst into a rendition of short melodies, like a singer warming up.

"That be Gabby. She comes 'round most every day." Neisha sprinkled some toast crumbs on the sill. Mia was intrigued. The bird seemed tame as a pet, and yet was wild and free, able to come and go as she pleased. Mia wished she could be free like that!

Bianca swept into the café from the back kitchen. "Why, I be thinkin' I was hearin' some chatterin', an' it ain't jus' Gabby."

"Hi, Bianca!" Mia gave her biggest smile.

"Why, Miss Mia, Neisha was sor' missin' you 'dis mownin'!" Bianca patted Mia's curls, her eyes smiling at her. Then she looked at Neisha and said, "I gotta be goin', for de bank be closin'. I hain't goin' tomorraw for de lines dey be long, long. Turs'day be payday in Bambarra."

"Go, Mama! Me and Mia will take care of the café for you, it be slow now anyways." Neisha threw a wet cloth at Mia. "We'll be gettin' tables ready for the evenin'-time customers."

"You is a good chile, Neisha girl, you is a good chile." Bianca put on her wide- brimmed hat topped with a parade of red and purple hibiscus blossoms. She opened the door and strutted out into the sunlight with her long skirt swirling around her ankles.

Neisha and Mia wiped down the tables with the big wet cloths. Neisha flipped on the radio and turned the volume way up. She sang while she worked. Mia tried to hum, but she found she couldn't reach half the notes. "You have a cool voice. Do you sing in your school choir?" Mia asked.

"I be singing mostly in the church choir, but lots of peoples sing there. The high school is where there be a real choir. They travel 'round to all the islands. But that be a long way off, cuz I don't know 'bout no high school."

"What do you mean, you don't know about high school?" Mia stopped cleaning tables and stared at Neisha in wonder. How could she not go to high school?

"My teacher, she say, I pass the examination, no problem. But there *be* a problem." Neisha sighed and said, "The high school be on the big island. I can't take a boat, that'd be too long to go back and forth every day. If I fly, I'd have to be a bird! You be needin' plenty money to fly."

"What do the other kids do?"

"They go live on the big island. My friend Tika went there. Her mama got a job at a big resort. So Tika can go to high school. Many people leave Bambarra to work on the big island."

"But what about your dad? Doesn't he live on the big island? Couldn't you stay with him?"

The Tea That Cures Everythin'!

"No, that won't be no good, he got another family on the big island. They be his inside family." Neisha busied herself with setting clean placemats on the tables.

"You mean your dad and mom are divorced? That happens all the time at home. The kids go back and forth between the mom and the dad for holidays and stuff."

"No, it ain't that. Lots of folks here has inside and outside families. We's an outside one. There can only be one inside family." Neisha passed the forks to Mia.

"So, you have brothers and sisters? Do you ever get to see them?"

"No, I never see them, they all live on other islands. My daddy, bein' a fisherman, he visit everybody." Neisha placed the knives and spoons around the tables.

"Does your dad come to Bambarra much?" Mia knew she was being nosy, but she couldn't help asking.

"Oh yes, he come round 'bout once a week, mostly Thursdays. He brings fresh grouper or snapper for the café. Mama grills what daddy brings with her special spice mix and makes him a good dinner when he comes. We sit around the table for hours and we jus' talk and laugh. On Christmas, he come to visit all his children, he gives each one a present all wrapped up in pretty paper. He's a good daddy. He's good to Mama and me." Neisha lined up the glasses wiping them with a soft, clean towel.

"My dad travels, too. He goes to lots of different countries on business, in Europe mostly. I miss him a ton when he goes away, but it is fun when he comes home." Mia felt her familiar homesickness. It made her stomach hurt. "I miss my mom, too. Especially now, cause she's sick."

"Why your mama sick? Why you not there with her?" Neisha stopped working to stare at Mia.

"I wanted to stay home, I didn't want to come here. I was supposed to go to camp with my best friend but..." Mia's voice quavered as she spoke. "Mom was so sick from her treatments that she couldn't even lift her head off of the pillow. It was her decision to send us here for the summer. She said I had to come to watch Jack, but he doesn't need watching." Mia's mouth felt dry. "My mom, she could do anything. Then one day she told us that she had a disease called Leukemia. The treatments that she has to take to make her better actually make her feel sick."

"Why those treatments make her sick? That don't make no good sense at all." Neisha shook her head from side to side.

"They have to kill the bad blood cells. That's what makes her sick. If they don't stop them from growing, the bad ones will take over and kill all the good ones. It's like her blood is at war with itself." Mia slumped down on the barstool.

Neisha tipped her head. "How they do that?"

"They use a chemical that poisons the bad cells."

"I hain't ever heard of poison makin' a person better. We got us a hospital, and sometimes peoples go in and they gets betta' and sometimes they don't. Some folks on the islands is still practicin' bush medicine."

"Bush medicine? What's that?" Mia wondered if it was like witch doctors or voodoo.

"We have a wise woman everybody calls Auntie Cecilia. When a body gets sick, she comes and makes them a tea. My Aunt Teeny was sick somethin' awful. She got real skinny, and couldn't eat nothin'. When she try to eat, it jus' come up again.

Auntie Cecilia bring her some of her tea. She say for Aunt Teeny to drink it three times a day. And she got right betta'! Aunt Teeny, she be makin' 90 years this July!"

"Do you think this tea could make my mom feel stronger?"

"Oh, yes, ma'am. This be the tea that cures everythin'!" Neisha placed her hands on her hips. "Yes, ma'am!"

"I've got to get me some of that tea!" Mia lit up. "Where do we find Auntie Cecilia?"

"She be livin' over on Pepper Cay. Your grandfather has him a boat, he can take you there."

"Gram would think it was stupid, she'd never approve of bush medicine. And Gramps wouldn't take us if Gram says no."

"How 'bout you rent a boat from the dive shop?"

Mia scrunched her forehead into a knot. "Darn! How could I charter a boat without my grandparents knowing about it? It would really have to be kept a secret. Anyhow, I'm sure it would cost a ton of money."

"You can help me wait tables. Sometimes the tourists leave good tips."

"I would love to wait tables! But don't you need your tips for yourself?" Mia wished there was a way it would work. If she could get the tea and her mom got stronger, she could come home! She could almost smell the marshmallows burning to a crispy golden brown over the open fire, with Sam and Ragsie by her side!

"I got no problem sharing tips. My friend Tika, she helped me wait tables, and we shared the tips right down the middle. 'Sides, it's more fun when two is waitin' tables than one!"

Mia groaned, "Gram will never let me wait tables. I'll have to get my mom's permission. She's the only one that can over-rule Gram! I gotta run to the library! I have e-mails to send!"

RED NAIL POLISH
Chapter 7

The Prince Albert Library stood silent and dark as Mia approached the enormous wooden doors. She tugged on the iron handle with more force than she needed to. The door swung outward, surprising her, in a wide arc. She was greeted by the cool stare of the librarian and a young boy standing on tiptoe in front of the checkout counter.

"Ma'am, you got *Horrible Harry*? He my fav-o-rite!"

The librarian busied herself finding the book for the boy. Mia slid to a desk holding two computers. She clicked on the mouse and its desktop came alive. It asked her to log in her password. *Shoot! I'll have to ask the librarian.*

"Good afternoon, Ma'am. May I use the computer to send some e-mails?"

"Good afternoon. Do you have a library card?" The librarian spoke with a crisp British accent. "If you are visiting, you must pay twenty dollars for a number, which will be refunded when you leave."

"I guess I'll need twenty dollars. I'm visiting my grandparents for the summer."

"Do your grandparents live here on Bambarra?"

"Yes. They are the Petersons, James and Irene."

"Irene Peterson is your grandmother?" The librarian smiled at Mia. "She is a fine lady. She helps us every winter with our book sale. She most certainly has a library card. You can use her number. Just one moment, I will look it up for you." Mia waited for the librarian to return; time was flying by and she was getting impatient. "Here is your number, just type it into the computer with your grandmother's name and you're all ready to go. Please say hello to her for me."

"Thanks, I will." Mia hungrily headed for the computer. She punched in her number and then hit the keys in a rapid fire to send an e-mail to Sam.

> *Hey Sam!*
>
> *How's Rags? I miss u and Ragamuffins so much. I can't wait for summer to be over. It is sooo boring here. No computers, TV, or DVD players, only a short wave radio that fuzzes. And I can't call cause my cell phone won't work here. Gram is always mad at me, she doesn't like me and Gramps spends all his time with Jack.*
>
> *The only good thing so far is that I met a girl who lives on the island, and her mom runs a café in town called The Green Flash. I'm helping her wait tables and stuff. We have a plan to get me back home soon. I can't tell u yet, cause it's a secret. But I will soon. Big hug to Rags. I hope you aren't having too much fun without me.*
>
> *Your best friend forever!*
> *Mia*

Mia hit the send button, and then, with equal speed, she set to work typing her next e-mail.

Hey Mom,

I hope you're feeling better. Is Dad home? I hope he doesn't have to go to Europe again. Is Aunt Cindy coming? Jack doesn't need me at all. There is not much for me to do here. I think it would be better for me to come home. I miss Rags and Sam. They are having a blast without me. My only good news is that I met a really nice girl, and her mom runs a café in town. I've been helping at the café. It is the only way to save me from dying of boredom! Would you tell Gram that it's okay for me to wait tables? If you give me permission she will have to let me. She is mad at me. I left the gate open and the donkeys got in the yard, you would think it was the end of the world. Her flowers will grow back.

I am working on a surprise for you! That's why I need to work at the café!

Please, please, please, write soon, and say YES to the café!

Love, Mia

Mia finished up her e-mails, thanked the librarian and headed out into the sunlight. It was so bright it made her eyes sting. She jogged down the street, staying in the dappled shade. The library was only a short way down the street from

The Green Flash Café. It would be easy for Mia to stick her head in, but now she felt it was time to head back home.

Mia hummed the song that Neisha had been singing as she entered the cool green courtyard. A butterfly landed on a pure white frangipani flower, the delicate flutter of its black and orange wings reminded Mia of miniature oriental fans.

Mia creaked through the donkey-battered kitchen door. "Hi Gram. Did Jack tell you I went to town to send some e-mails to Mom and Sam? The librarian let me use your number. She said to say hi."

"Jack told me that you went to The Green Flash Café."

"I just stopped by on my way to the library; I wanted to say hi to Neisha. She showed me how to set up the tables and fill the ketchup bottles."

"I will not permit you to go there anymore. It's not proper for a young lady to be hanging around a café with a bar in it. And worse yet, to work in one!"

"But I *want* to help out. I want to wait tables and make tips. It will give me something to *do* this summer."

"Mia, you don't know what it's like to live on an island. People talk, and they will talk if they know my granddaughter is hanging around that Green Flash Café and working for tips!"

"I've already sent an e-mail to Mom. She'll say it's okay, she'll give me her permission!" Mia's anger was rising like mercury in a thermometer, ready to burst.

"Mia, don't you make anything harder for your mother than it already is. You should be spending more time with Jack. That's what your mother and your father would want."

Mia felt like she was suffocating. "I hate you! You don't know anything about my mother! My mom would want me to make friends and have fun. I wish it was you that was sick, not my mom!"

Mia ran to the shelter of her room and slammed the door. The sobs came in big waves, racking her body, draining all of the energy out of her like a tidal river sucking her downstream.

Gradually the sobs slowed. She was exhausted. Every night since her mom got sick, Mia woke up in a sweat with the same nightmare. It made her nauseous to think about it. Her head hurt and so did her cried-out eyes. She tiptoed out of her bedroom to wash her face. The towel she used was rough from being dried in the hot sun. It scratched her face and made her cheeks rosy. It felt good.

Mia slipped back into her room, hoping Jack wouldn't hear her. She didn't want to see his toothy smile. There, on her desk, was the red fingernail polish that her mom had given her. She scooped up the bottle of polish and plopped herself on the bed. She wiggled her toes and stretched them out as she brushed the red polish over each toenail. She thought how much fun it would be to share the polish with Neisha. She wanted to ask Neisha to braid her hair in tight rows like hers. Her hair was turning in to a mop of frizz. It was sticky and full of mats like a rats nest; she could barely get a brush through it. She was lost in thought, bristling about how Gram couldn't keep her from waiting tables at the Green Flash. And somehow, somehow... she would get to Pepper Cay to get Auntie Cecilia's tea for her mom so she could go back home...

Bam! Her door suddenly burst wide open, jamming the doorknob into the wall. Mia's heart leapt. The nail polish flew out of her hand, spinning high up into the air. It landed on its side, smack dab in the middle of Gram's quilt. Mia lunged to grab the bottle before it emptied itself, but it was too late. Jack stood in the doorway, grinning. "Ready to go to the beach, like you promised?"

Mia's eyes narrowed to thin slits. "You rat! You traitor! You told Gram I went to The Green Flash Café."

"I didn't tell her nothin', nothin' she didn't already know." Jack scurried into the safety of the courtyard.

Mia looked down at the quilt. There was a deep blob of red, right where the bottle had landed. "Shoot! It will never come out!" She searched for the bottle of nail polish remover. She poured the evil smelling solution on the toe of a clean white sock and dabbed at the red puddle. It lightened a little at first. But, the more she worked on it, the larger it grew. It spread wider and wider still, matching the sinking feeling that was growing in the pit of her stomach.

BROTHERLY LOVE
Chapter 8

The popping sound from the tin roof expanding in the early morning sun was ringing in Mia's ears. It sounded like a flamenco dancer tapping her shoes. She plopped her pillow over her head, but she couldn't breathe. She rolled over and stretched from the tops of her toes to the tips of her fingers. She was awake earlier than usual. She had had that bad dream again. She was sticky with sweat. The memory of her words with Gram yesterday hung heavy on her conscience. She tried to shrug it off, but it wouldn't leave her. And there was something else that was bugging her, but she wasn't sure what. Then she remembered...Oh god! The nail polish on the quilt.

She rolled herself out of bed in one swift motion, landing on her feet. As she threw on her cut-off jeans and T-shirt, Mia decided she'd slip out and take a walk down to the beach before breakfast. Maybe it would help her cool off. She was still ripping mad at Jack for telling Gram that she was at the café.

Mia tiptoed through the hallway, not wanting to wake Jack. But his door was wide open, so she peeked in. It looked like a battle had taken place! The pillow was jammed in between the bed and the wall and the sheet was drawn halfway across the room and lay twisted on the floor. Jack was gone.

Mia slipped out of the house and down the path to the beach. The early morning sun rose out of the sea like a fire-breathing dragon. She hardly noticed the bright clusters of beach buttercups tipping their faces toward her as she passed. The sea wind caressed her, making her unruly curls dance. She followed the vines of purple morning glories that twisted and tumbled down toward the white sand. Her mind churned. *Why had everything turned upside down?* Even if she could get the tea, would it really help her mom? Was she going on a silly wild goose chase? And how was she ever going to get the red blob out of the quilt before Gram found it? And Gram! How could she ever face Gram after blowing up at her last night?

The beach appeared to be empty except for a pair of osprey diving for their breakfast. Their shrill cry made Mia stop and take notice. She watched how the birds soared, riding the air currents without moving a feather. Then, suddenly, one plunged straight down with unnerving accuracy, and then took flight with a silver fish grasped in its talons. Mia walked toward the northern point of the island. She spotted a big driftwood log that had washed up from the sea, cutting off one section of the beach. In the middle of the log was a lump. A lump all wrapped in a beach towel.

"Hey, Jack. Why are you up so early?"

He didn't answer. He just pulled the towel tighter around himself, covering his head and face.

"What's the matter, little brother? I didn't throw your camera in the ocean yet!" Mia teased as she climbed onto the log.

"Go away!" Jack sniffled into the towel.

"You want to go look for footprints? Or maybe we can find a message in a bottle?" Mia leaned closer to him, wondering what could be the problem.

"No! You never want to be with me. You leave me alone, while you go and have fun at the café." Jack's whole body shook. He was crying, hard.

Mia started to put her arm around him, but he shoved her away. Surprised, she scooted backwards a few inches, giving him more space.

Half of the towel slipped from his face. Mia gasped. It looked like he had been crying all night. His face was red and puffy, his eyes, magnified by his glasses, were almost swollen shut, and his nose was red and running. He gulped some air and looked away from her.

"Jack, what's the matter?" She couldn't believe he was that mad at her.

"I miss M-m-mom and D-d-dad," Jack stuttered.

"Oh Jack, I do too. We'll go home soon. Maybe we won't have to stay the whole summer." Mia was trying to convince herself, as well as Jack.

"I want to go ho-ho-home now. I-I-I'm so afraid that Mom will d-d-die and we'll never . . . " Jack choked down fresh sobs. Mia took hold of his arms and forced him to look at her. She felt his bony body shiver.

"Jack, Mom won't die."

"You don't know! Mom is sick real b-b-bad. Dad told Gram that it's the bad kind of leukemia." Jack hiccupped.

"Yes, Jack. Mom *is* very sick. But I have a secret plan," Mia whispered.

"A plan? What kind of plan?" Jack wiggled out of Mia's grasp.

"Neisha and I are working on getting something that will help Mom get stronger. We still have a few kinks to work out yet." She probably shouldn't have been telling Jack, but at least he was perking up.

"You can tell me; I promise I won't tell. I want Mom to get better more than anything!" Jack's old self was coming back.

"How can I trust you, when you've already proven yourself to be a traitor?" Mia pointed her finger at Jack's red nose.

"I didn't tell. Gram knew anyways. She asked me where you went, but she already knew." Jack blinked his red, swollen eyelids.

"She already knew? How could she know?"

"Her friend that she plays cards with, you know that Mrs. Jones with the big nose, she saw you go into the café. She called Gram on the telephone. I heard the whole thing." Jack was very convincing. "Anyways, this is different."

"No, it's not different. A traitor is a traitor!" Mia shook her finger at him. "But, I will think about it, if you promise on your Scout's Honor. If you break your promise, I will make you wish you were never born. And I'm not kidding!"

"I promise, I promise, Scout's Honor!" Jack flashed the scout sign at Mia, with his three fingers up. "What's the plan?"

"Well, Neisha knows a wise woman who makes a tea that cures everything. No one she treats dies! We just have to figure how to get to Pepper Cay where she lives, so we can buy some tea from her."

"You mean you need a boat to get there? How are you going to get a boat?" Jack rubbed his head with his knuckles.

"Neisha and I were going to save up our tips from working at the café. Then we could hire a boat to take us there. But now Gram is wrecking everything. She says I can't wait tables."

Jack scrunched up his face, thinking. Suddenly, he lit up like a light bulb without a shade.

"I got an idea! Why not borrow Gramps' boat? You know, when he takes his nap. I can drive it. Really, I know how."

"That's a stupid idea. It's a long trip to Pepper Cay, much farther than Little Turtle. We need to hire a boat driver."

"I can do it, Mia. I know I can! Gramps has taken me out a bunch of times. He always lets me do some of the driving. And I can dock the boat myself and everything."

"That's enough about it for now. But don't forget, you gave me your Scout's Honor you wouldn't say anything." Mia squeezed her eyes into thin slits as she looked at him.

"I won't forget! Let's go. I'm so hungry, I could eat a horse!"

"How about a donkey?" Mia chuckled.

"Lasso me up a fat one!" Jack was smiling again.

Mia and Jack rounded the crest of the dunes to the beach. From a distance, she could see the silhouette of Gram carrying a tray of orange juice and fresh fruit to the terrace.

"Oh shoot, I'm a dead donkey when Gram finds out about the quilt! See ya later, I gotta go hide it!" Mia raced back to her room, taking the roundabout way to avoid Gram. There waiting for her was the quilt. The stain had dried and it looked, to Mia, like it was there for good. She rolled it up in a ball, making sure the stain wasn't visible, and shoved it into the bottom drawer of the rattan dresser. She needed time. She needed to get back to the library to get her answer from her mom.

She decided she couldn't face Gram, so she snuck out of her bedroom and headed for the gate and the road to town.

RASTA MAN RAFTARI
Chapter 9

Hey Sam!

I got your e-mail. Glad to hear Rags is being a good boy. I miss my Muffins soooo much. I miss you too. I hate it here. Things are a terrible mess. I told you about the café. Gram says I can't go there anymore. She thinks it looks bad to her snooty friends. I am going to ask Mom, she's cool and she'll understand.

Hugs and hugs to you and Rags,
Your best friend always and forever!
Mia

Hi Mom,

I didn't get an e-mail from you. I need to hear back from you!
Did Gram call you last night? She is not being fair at all.
Gram says I can't work at the café because it doesn't look good to her friends. Neisha is really nice

and I need a friend, so please say yes. I could make some tips, and it would be so much fun and make the summer go by quicker. I know you will understand. I won't do anything to mess up, I promise. I will even bring Jack with me, sometimes.

Please say yes!!

Love,
Mia

Mia read over her e-mail to her mother twice and then crossed her fingers as she hit send. She pondered for a moment: what would she do if her mom said no? She decided not to think about it. She would have to come back later to get her mom's answer.

Neisha hadn't been sitting on the wall when Mia went to the library, but luckily she was there now.

"Hey, I'm glad to see you."

"I be here waitin' for you." Neisha's smile lit up her whole face.

"I'm afraid I have some bad news." Mia frowned.

"Let's go inside where it be nice and cool."

"That's the bad news. My grandmother won't allow me to go inside the café. C'mon let's go for a walk on the beach."

Neisha hopped down from her perch, scraping her jeans on the white limestone as she slid down. She gave her backside a quick brush-off. "Okay! We go walkin'!"

Neisha hollered to her mom that she'd be back in time to help with lunch.

"Why you not allowed inside the café?" she asked with concern.

"Well, Gram is worried about what her snooty friends might say if they saw me working at the café. She thinks it will make her look bad. But I sent an e-mail to my mom asking for her permission. I even told her I would bring Jack along some of the time. I thought that might help her say yes."

"Yes sir, that'd be bad news. What we gonna do if your mama say no?"

"She will say yes, she is totally different than Gram."

"Okay, I'll be savin' my tips for Auntie Cecilia's tea." Neisha sounded determined.

"You're a real friend, Neisha!" Mia slipped off her sandals and let her toes feel the powdery white sand. Together, they ran up to the crashing waves and then retreated quickly. They laughed at themselves and then did it again.

"Oh look! It's that man riding Sandy," Mia said, pointing. "Do you know him?"

"He be Raftari, my daddy knows him. My daddy, he knows everybody!"

"I met him the first day I came to Bambarra. He offered me a ride on Sandy."

"She be a fine horse. You can ride her, she be good, not like some who rub you off into the prickly pears."

"Wow, I would love to ride her. I love horses! Let's go!"

The girls waved to Raftari. He grinned from ear to ear when he saw them. Sandy looked happy, too. She followed his lead and headed down from the cobblestone road to the sandy beach. Her hooves sank into the soft sand, but once she reached the water's edge, the sand was firm as a road. She trotted along with her blonde mane blowing in the wind, revealing a perfect white star on her forehead.

"Good morning, my bee-u-tiful ladies. Maybe you take Sawndee' for a ride today?" He patted Sandy's neck. She snorted and shook her head up and down as if in agreement.

"Good mornin', Raftari. This be Mia. She come all the way from Boston. She like to ride Sandy, but we got no money." Neisha held out both hands, palms face up.

"Okay, mon, that be jus' okay. Sawndee' ride ladies togedder. Maybe some peoples sees how gen-teel she be and dey wants to ride Sawndee' too." He slid off the horse and put his hands together in a stirrup shape. Neisha hopped up first, swinging her leg high over Sandy's back, and landing right in the middle of the blanket. Mia mounted next, fitting in easily behind Neisha. Raftari handed the rope to Neisha and said, "Pull de rope des way and she go des way. Pull de rope dat way, she go dat way. Click to go, and jus' give her gen-teel pat on her be-hine'. You like to go fast use de foots and kick her both sides. She like to run. Sawndee' will stop when you pull back de rope. Okay, mon, she go na!" He gave Sandy a slap on the rump and she broke into a frisky trot.

Mia held on tight to Neisha, trying not to bump into her. Soon the two riders were in rhythm with Sandy. The turquoise water shimmered and the wind cooled them. Mia felt all her cares melting away. The girls rode up the shoreline and all along Front Street where the tourists walked. They waved at the ladies with sunglasses and straw-visors, and men with big bellies and tight t-shirts who clicked their cameras at them.

A group of boys perched on the dock had fishing lines tied onto small, round weights. Mia was intrigued by how they threw the lines into the water and then methodically hauled them back in. One of the boys turned to watch them approach. He motioned to the others, and several of them ran out in front of Sandy. They waved their arms and made high-pitched whooping noises. Neisha clicked her tongue and gave Sandy a kick with both of her feet. Sandy, happy to run, broke into a canter, plowing right through the surprised boys. Mia and Neisha laughed as the boys scrambled to save themselves from Sandy's heavy hooves.

"What were those boys trying to do?" Mia shouted into Neisha's ear.

"They try an scare her, so she throw us off. Dey be rude boys!" Neisha spat out the words.

"We showed them!" Mia yelled into the wind.

The girls circled back, and this time the boys stayed far out of their path. Raftari was waiting for them with a couple of sunburned tourists. The girls quickly dismounted. They watched with amusement as Raftari ceremoniously presented Sandy with a delicious-looking carrot. He sang a sailor's ditty as he pulled out a metal bowl and canteen from his satchel and filled it to the top with fresh water.

"Sawndee' give you gen-teel ride, okay? Dese folks want to ride Sawndee'. Dey see my bee-u-tiful ladies, an dey ask to ride Sawndee'. My ladies, dey be good for bee's-nez." Raftari bowed to the girls.

"Thanks for the ride, Sandy!" Mia rubbed her velvet nose. "Glad we could help drum up some costumers," she said, smiling at Raftari.

"You welcome, na. Okay, bye bye."

He made a stirrup with his hands and gave instructions to the next rider. He tucked a ten-dollar bill into his satchel as Sandy trotted down the beach.

Mia walked with Neisha as far as the library.

"I hope your mama be feelin' betta', and she be sayin' yes."

"Thanks, wish me luck!" Mia, still exhilarated from the ride, did a little dance step into the library.

To her great dismay, there were three boys crowded around a computer playing some sort of game. The other computer had a sign on it saying "out of order." Darn! Who knew how long these kids would be? Frustrated, she huffed out of the library, planning to come back right after lunch. She was mighty hungry after skipping breakfast. Mia felt queasy about going back to the house, though. She'd have to say she was sorry to Gram for what she said last night. Mia worried that Gram might even be mean enough to ground her, and that would ruin everything!

Mia managed to push all the uncomfortable thoughts out of her mind and concentrate on her ride on Sandy. Oh, how she wished she could have her own horse. Neisha had told her, "The horses that run wild, is wild, nobody does own them. All you got to do is put some jam on a piece of bread and hold it out on your hand, flat. The wild horse will come and take it because they be lovin' sweets. Then, quick as lightning, you jus' slip a rope round their neck. You be the owner of a horse!" Mia daydreamed about catching a young horse and training it herself. She would feed it apples and carrots and brush its soft blonde mane every day.

Mia made it back to the house just in time for lunch. She slid into her assigned chair at the terrace table and gave Jack a wink. He acknowledged her by cracking his knuckles on both hands.

Gram carried a tray stacked full of sandwiches, followed by Gramps with cold sodas. Mia was starved! She spotted a plate layered with homemade brownies and ripe peaches. Her stomach rumbled in anticipation.

Gram laid the tray on the table. She cleared her throat and looked at Mia. "I took the truck downtown to the post office this morning. Did I see you riding horseback with Bianca's daughter?"

"Her name is Neisha. We went for a walk on the beach and we met Raftari and he let us ride Sandy. I would love to have a horse! Neisha says all you have to do is..."

Gram cut her off mid-sentence. "Mia do you know who that man is? He's a Rasta man." Gram had a pulsing vein in the middle of her forehead.

"What's a Rasta man?"

"A Rasta man is a person from Jamaica that takes drugs for his religion! He sells rides on that poor horse of his to make the money he needs to buy his marijuana."

"But that can't be true, he let us ride for free. And he takes good care of Sandy. She's way better off than the wild horses that get cut up in the bush and have to scrounge for fresh water to drink." Mia could feel her temperature rising. She had to keep calm or she would make matters even worse, like getting grounded.

"Horses are dangerous animals. Do you know there are more horseback riding accidents than car accidents? I can't believe your parents let you ride horses at all. You could easily fall off and land on your head. I read in the papers about this young girl who was kicked and had to have a steal plate put in her head. She was never the same after that!"

Mia remained silent as her Grandmother droned on and on. How could her grandfather stand all these lectures? Jack wasn't listening; he was too busy gorging himself. *Ugh*. Mia was exasperated by all of them. She was getting desperate. She had to get her mother's answer!

BEWARE OF THE CALM DAY
Chapter 10

Mia stared at the computer screen, the letters fuzzing before her eyes. "Play by your grandmother's rules. It is just for a little longer. I need you to be brave." This was her mother's answer? "Spend more time with Jack; he needs you." She wanted to scream! She had to find a way around Gram's rules. She had to find a way to Pepper Cay.

Mia walked the long way home. She didn't want to go past the café or she'd have to tell Neisha the bad news. She found herself walking in the direction of the dive shop. It was just a little further down the road. A hand-painted sign was propped up against the front of the shop. It listed trips to Little Turtle Cay, to feed the stingrays and for whale watching. No mention of Pepper Cay. Mia figured she might as well go in and ask. As she opened the door, a bell tinkled. A lady in a pink t-shirt with sun-bleached hair popped out of the back room.

"Hi, hon. How can I help you?"

"I was just wondering if there are any boat trips to Pepper Cay?"

"It would have to be a special charter. How many are in your party?"

"Just two, or, um, maybe three." Mia thought about Jack. "Does it matter how many?"

"Well, it's three hundred dollars to charter a boat for the day. If you get a bigger group, you can reduce the price per person."

"Oh, that's okay. I was just curious. Pepper Cay sounded like a neat place."

"Yes, Pepper Cay is very special. It rains more there, so it's filled with all kinds of rare plants and flowers. It's certainly worth the trip. Why don't I take down your name and phone number? I'll give you a call if someone else wants to go."

"Well, um, you don't need to call. I was just curious." Mia pushed the door open and escaped into the bright sunlight. Three hundred dollars! That was impossible! There had to be another way. Jack's idea sounded better by the minute.

Mia turned around and headed back toward the Green Flash Café. Neisha was there, sitting on the wall. Mia poured out the whole story. At the end she blurted out her new plan: "Jack will drive the boat!"

Neisha looked at her toes. "Maybe I could ask my daddy? He has him a good fishin' boat, and he knows all the islands. He say someday he will take me on his boat, maybe this be the day. He will get us safe to Pepper Cay."

"My Gram doesn't have Internet but she sure does have radar! If she finds out she'll wreck everything! Will your dad keep a secret?"

"My daddy be tellin' your granddaddy." Neisha shook her head. "He'd not be takin' you and me out for a trip to Pepper

Cay just to buy tea, he'd be fishin' too. My daddy, no way he be takin' you on the boat all day without checkin' with your grands."

"That won't work! If Gramps knows he'll tell Gram and she'll put a stop to it, I know she will. It looks like the only way we can keep Gram from knowing is to sneak Gramps' boat when they are sleeping. Jack can drive us straight to Pepper Cay and back."

Neisha looked uncertain. "You say Jack is ten years old? How he be drivin' a boat by himself?"

"Don't worry! He can do it! He drove home from Turtle Cay."

"Pepper Cay be farther than Turtle Cay."

"He can do it! He has driven the boat a bunch of times with Gramps and he says he knows how to dock it too. Anyways, it is our only chance! I'll let you know if tomorrow is clear. We'll leave right after lunch when my grandparents are sawing logs."

"Sawing logs? What kind of logs they be sawing?"

Mia laughed. "That means sleeping! We'll take off when my grandparents are sleeping, right after lunch."

Neisha looked solemn as she waved goodbye to Mia.

Mia rushed back to the house. She found Jack sitting in the garage alone, working on the model ship.

"Hey, Jack. You want to walk down to the beach with me?"

"Where've ya been?" Jack didn't look at Mia, but kept working on his ship. His lower lip stuck out in a pout.

"Makin' plans that include you! C'mon. I'll tell you all about it when no one can hear us." Jack put down his model and scurried to catch up.

As soon as they hit the beach Mia began to give Jack the lowdown.

"We'll sail tomorrow, if the sea is calm. Neisha will meet us down by the dock. We'll leave a note for Gram and Gramps. I'll say that you and I have gone to town to help shelve books at the library and that we won't be back till dinner. If I say that I'm taking you with me, Gram is less likely to suspect anything. We'll sail to Pepper Cay, find Auntie Cecilia, buy the tea, and return before we are missed."

"But what about the lady at the library? She's friends with Gram."

"It's a risk we'll have to take! Anyways, if Gram checks on us, we'll be long gone."

The next morning broke gray and drizzling rain. By afternoon there were high winds strong enough to rip the clothes right off of the clothesline. Mia was disheartened with the weather, and to make matters worse, Gram watched her every move, like a hawk hoping to catch mouse. Mia figured that she must be suspicious of something. Mia decided to skip her trip into town to see Neisha. She would know it was not a sailing day.

The next day, large waves rolled in with white foam caps that hit the beach like thunder. Mia and Jack worked on putting together a thousand piece puzzle, the only puzzle Gram and Gramps had. Unfortunately, it was a picture of boats in a Caribbean harbor. Mia's spirits sank lower and her nerves were on edge. Jack bit his nails and kept going into the kitchen for chips and crunchy things. He smacked his lips while he ate.

"Close your mouth, you sound like a chimpanzee." Mia wanted to punch him!

Beware of the Calm Day

By the third day, the sea settled, but not enough for a small boat to attempt to sail. Mia couldn't force herself to play one more round of crazy eights with Jack or suffer through one more dastardly game of chess. She dug out the rest of her summer reading books and hit the hammock with a long sigh.

Thursday morning arrived as gentle as a lamb. Right after breakfast, when Gram and Gramps were taking their swim, Mia slipped out the gate, closing it tight behind her, and jogged toward town. She had to get the word to Neisha that today was the day. She sprinted past Crabtree Corner and spotted Raftari and Sandy along the road. Two skinny tourist boys with baseball caps were waiting for a ride. Mia couldn't pass by Sandy without giving her a warm nuzzle.

"Hi, Sandy! How's my girl?"

One of the boys made a feeble effort to pat Sandy on the neck. The muscles in Sandy's neck quivered as if she were ridding herself of a biting fly.

"Sawndee' be crawnkee' today. She no like it when de wind is so steel."

"Oh, but the weather is beautiful today. The water is so calm it's like glass. On a clear day like this you could sail forever."

"Beware of de calm day, my bee-u-tiful lady! Dey can be troubles comin'. Ya grands not goin' out sailin to-dee'?" He scrunched up his face with concern.

"Oh, no, not today." Mia thought for a moment about his warning but decided it was nonsense. The storm was over. In her enthusiasm, she blurted out, "Hey, Raftari, have you ever been to Pepper Cay?"

"Mon, I be born dere!" He made a stirrup with his hands, hoisting one of the lads onto Sandy's back.

"Really! Do you know an Auntie Cecilia?"

"Auntie Cecilia? Auntie Cecilia?" He handed the rope reins to the boy. "She be right dere, mon, she be right dere, da day I be born."

"You mean she was the nurse?"

"No, mon. Auntie Cecilia ain't no nurse. Auntie Cecilia she be de bush doctaw! She takin' care of all de folks when dey be needin' her hep. She be a wise woman." Raftari took the ten-dollar bill the boy pulled out of his pocket.

Mia needed him to verify what Neisha had said about the tea. She needed proof that it would really help her mom. "Does she really have a tea that cures everything?"

"I do believe she does brew many, many teas. She brew de special tea that she be makin' when folks is poorly. When dey drink dis tea, it be makin' folks feel right betta."

He gave Sandy a slap on her rump. Sandy whinnied, shaking her head from left to right. She stretched her neck to chew on a dried clump of donkey thistle, refusing to budge.

"Sorry, mon. Sawndee' don' wan' to ride to-dee'. She da boss, mon, she da boss."

Mia watched as he pulled the paper bill out of his satchel and returned it to the surprised boy.

Mia said goodbye and ran to find Neisha, her head spinning. Home, here I come! Sam and Rags, here I come! Summer camp, here I come!

Mia scooted behind the café to the back window. She whistled. Neisha poked her head out.

"Hey, girl! Today is the day! Two o'clock at the dock." Mia felt giddy.

"Okay, I be comin'. But it sure be plenty, plenty hot today. I be bringin' some cold water for us." Neisha wiped the perspiration from her forehead with the back of her hand and disappeared from view.

AUNTIE CECILIA
Chapter 11

L unch was long and painful. The food stuck in Mia's throat. Jack piled his plate up high and ate like he would never see food again.

Gram chatted at them. "Our walk on the beach this morning was quite interesting; Gramps and I were accompanied by a lemon shark. We walked along the edge in the shallow water and he swam just a few feet from us. He must have been four or five feet long!" Mia winced at the thought of sharks in the nearby water.

"Do lemon sharks attack people?" Jack asked with his mouth full of food.

Gramps joined in good naturedly, "They don't normally. But if you're swimming and you see one, you should get out of the water. No need to tempt fate."

"Oh, James, you know they are harmless, don't frighten the children, they'll be afraid to swim in the ocean. The big hammerheads are all safely out past the reefs." Gram began stacking up the finished plates. "Mia, you've hardly eaten a thing!" Dark wrinkles spread over her forehead as she inspected Mia's plate.

"I'm not really hungry right now. I'll save it for later." Mia's stomach rebelled at the thought of food.

After lunch was cleared and the dishes were washed and put away, Gram and Gramps settled in for their afternoon nap. Mia and Jack jumped into action. They smeared sun block all over themselves, especially on Jack's nose. Mia grabbed a couple of beach towels and her iPod. She stuffed several five-dollar bills into the pocket of her backpack, hoping that would be enough to cover the cost of the tea. She scratched out a note in big letters on the kitchen counter. That done, Mia and Jack snuck down the driveway to the gate, being careful to lock it behind them.

They hiked the short distance to the dock. The boat was sitting there waiting for them. Mia checked the life jackets and all seemed ready. Except that Neisha was missing. Five, ten, fifteen precious minutes went by and no sign of Neisha. *Oh, please come, Neisha! Please come soon! How will I find Auntie Cecilia without you?*

Mia was just about ready to jump out of her skin when she saw Neisha running toward the dock like a bounding gazelle. Tucked in her arms were three bottles of water.

Neisha hopped into the boat, dropping the water bottles into Mia's hands. "Sorry! Mama had me clean up afta' lunch. I got some customers who ain't got nothin' betta' to do than jus' be sittin' there and gabbin' all day long." Neisha made talking signs with her hands.

"It's okay. Let me introduce you to Captain Jack."

Neisha held out her hand.

Jack gave her hand a yank and chirped, "Glad ta meet cha!"

Mia looked anxiously around to see if anyone had noticed them. But not one person was to be seen. "Okay Jack, anchors away!"

Jack flipped the fan switch on and proceeded with the start up. He cranked the throttle forward twice, put it in neutral, and then turned the motor on. He lowered the motor and pressed the throttle forward into gear. They were soon chugging along the inlet, heading toward the passage to the sea. The sky was deep blue with just a wisp of white clouds.

The water was smooth as glass as they rounded Little Turtle Cay. Jack skirted the *Dragonfly* past the channel between Iguana Cay and Little Turtle Cay. Circling around Iguana Cay, the *Dragonfly* was positioned in a direct line toward Pepper Cay. Mia was reassured by Jack's competence; he drove the boat as well as Gramps. She began to relax.

"Look, a flying fish!" Jack pointed to a rainbow-colored fish with wings that flew right alongside the boat. As the fish melted back into the water, another emerged, taking its place like magic.

Neisha cried out, "I ain't never seen a fish fly!"

Jack turned from the wheel to look at Neisha. "Mia said your dad was a fisherman. You must see tons of things out in the ocean, like sharks and whales."

"No, I don't go fishin' with my daddy. He promises, but he not be takin' me. He be teachin' the boys to fish. I guess he don't need to bother teachin' a girl to fish."

"You got brothers? Where are they hidin'? I sure would like to find some guy friends."

"Ya, I got me some brothers. But I don't see them; they mostly be livin' on the big island."

"But why do they live on the big island when you live on Bambarra...?"

"Never you mind, Jack." Mia cut in. "Just drive the boat." She squinted her eyes searching for any sign of land. "Hey, land ho! There she is, Pepper Cay!" Mia watched with great anticipation as the distant speck grew into an island. Soon she could see the shape of a dock waiting for them.

"Wahoo! We made it!" Jack crowed.

Jack drove the boat up to the dock without a hitch. He ordered the two girls to prepare for landing. Then he jumped onto the dock and tied the boat up with a fancy seaman's knot.

Mia hopped onto the dock, followed by Neisha. "Stay here and mind the boat, Jack. Don't go anywhere! We'll get the tea and get back as quick as we can." Mia gave Jack the *I mean it* look.

"Hey, how come I don't get to come, too?" Jack looked dejected.

"You stay put and watch the boat! We'll be as quick as we can!"

"That stinks! Why am I always the one left behind?"

"Because you're the captain and you can't leave your boat!" Mia turned her attention from Jack to Neisha, "How do we find Auntie Cecilia?" Mia looked around, trying to get a feel for this island. She had an uneasy feeling in the pit of her stomach.

Neisha was calm. "We jus' go to town and ask for Auntie Cecilia, no problem. Everybody, they be knowin' the wise woman!"

Just past the dock there was a signpost with an arrow pointing in the direction of town. The two girls broke into a jog, passing donkeys and roosters just like in Bambarra. But it was different, too; wild flowers bloomed everywhere, and the bush itself was tall and lush. The road taking them to town meandered past square stucco houses painted in brilliant shades of yellows, greens, and blues. The roofs were made of corrugated tin with gutters that flowed into cement basins to catch the rainfall. Mia laughed at treasures that must have washed on shore from the sea. They jogged past a house that had an old diver's suit, complete with helmet, propped up alongside a hammock made of fishing nets the color of limes and oranges.

Mia blinked as she ran past a church that glowed with newly whitewashed walls. Along the highest peak, a large white cross cut a sharp silhouette against the brilliant blue sky. The road was absent of all vehicles, moving or parked. Mia never once saw a traffic light or a stop sign. The only person she saw was a man on a bicycle who nodded a friendly, "Good afta'noon," as he pedaled by.

Mia and Neisha slowed their pace as they reached what appeared to be a small village center. A tall, stately lady glided toward them from the opposite side of the road. She was dressed in a flowing black skirt tied neatly at the waist. A woven shawl was wrapped around her broad shoulders and pinned together with a large safety pin. She wore leather sandals covered with fine white sand. She held her head high and carried a black umbrella that cast a dark shadow over her face. She nodded at the girls.

"Good afta'noon."

"Good afta'noon." Neisha nodded back. "We come from Bambarra and we be lookin' for Auntie Cecilia. My friend, she be needin' her tea."

"Why you be needin' her tea? Auntie Cecilia sure not be messin' around with no silly girls."

"Mia's mama, she be sick real bad."

"What kind of sick she be?" The woman asked skeptically.

Mia spoke up, "My mom has a disease called leukemia. We came to get the tea that cures everything!"

"Well na, Auntie Cecilia does got a tea that cures jus' bout everythin'. You jus' follow Mary." She strode along the road with such long strides that Mia and Neisha had to stretch their legs to keep up with her. They marched like soldiers in a line, past tiny houses that spread farther and farther apart. They finally approached a lavender cottage with a white limestone wall wrapped around it. Perched on top of the wall was a perfect line of conch shells, each one painted a matching shade of purple. Inside the walls, profuse blossoms burst forth in brilliant hues of purples, blues, and pinks.

This must be Auntie Cecilia's cottage! Mia thought. But their leader swept past the cottage and walked diagonally across the road. A sign, painted the same purple as the conch shells, hung over the open door of a plain white stucco building. Mia read aloud, "HATTIE'S VARIETY STORE."

"Good afta'noon, Hattie. We be lookin' for Auntie Cecilia. She be in?" Mary stepped into the darkened shop, placing her open umbrella against the door.

"Yes, ma'am. Dis afta'-noon' her door be open. She be in."

She smiled at the girls. Mia liked how her wrinkles smiled too.

Mary thanked Hattie, picked up her umbrella, and marched back outside. Mia and Neisha followed her back out into the blinding sunlight.

Mia felt as if they were being taken on a sacred pilgrimage as they traveled down a long, winding path that led to a stone fence with a wooden gate. Beyond the closed gate was a simple stone house with its front door flung wide open, as if inviting them to enter. The windows on either side of the door were framed with green shutters propped open by sticks. White lacy curtains billowed through the open windows, making the house feel cozy and lived in. On the far side of the house was a garden separated here and there by a foot-worn path. There were rows and rows of plants that Mia couldn't even begin to name. Some had dainty purple and yellow flowers and some looked like what Mia would normally have considered weeds, or what Neisha had called just plain bush. Mia wondered if this was where the magic tea came from.

"Auntie Cecilia's door be open." Mary opened the gate and called to the house, "Auntie Cecilia, it be Mary, and I be havin' two girls with me."

Mary made no move to enter, but stood just inside the gate. Mia was so nervous she was ready to jump out of her skin. She held her breath. It seemed endless, and the silence echoed in her ears. Then, finally, she heard a rustling and clinking within the house, followed by the sounds of chairs or tables being dragged across a wooden floor. An aged but friendly voice called to them, "Come! Come inside. I will make us some tea."

Mia's skin prickled into goose bumps as they entered the house single file. There, sitting on a chair of woven sea grass, was Auntie Cecilia. Her weathered face crinkled into a welcoming smile. "Good afta'noon, Mary. You bring me young visitors!"

Neisha stepped forward, offering her hand. Auntie Cecilia patted her hand warmly, then, still holding on to Neisha's hand, she reached for Mia's. Auntie Cecilia squeezed it tightly and gazed deep into Mia's blue eyes. Mia wondered if she was casting a spell on her. She was unused to holding peoples hands, and wanted to pull her hand away. A gnawing feeling grew in her stomach. Auntie Cecilia was missing most of her teeth, and around her neck she wore a large silver chain adorned with buttons and safety pins in all shapes and sizes. In the center, there hung a cluster of keys that dangled down like charms. The keys ranged in size from large skeleton keys to the tiniest diary keys. They clinked together as Auntie Cecilia moved. A purple scarf tied around her head allowed a few wisps of white hair to escape. Her eyes were clear and deep brown with crinkles on the sides. They mesmerized Mia, penetrating to her innermost being. She shivered.

"I will brew us some tea. While I be busy doin' that, you tell me why you have come to visit Auntie Cecilia."

"Yes, yes, the girls, they can be tellin' you why they come. I be on my way na'. Good afta'noon, Auntie Cecilia, good afta'noon girls." Mary nodded her head and walked through the open door, retrieving her open umbrella.

Neisha called out, "Thanks, Mary! Thanks for helpin' us find Auntie Cecilia." Then she turned to the wise woman. "I am Neisha, and this be my friend Mia. She come all the way from Boston. Her mama be real sick."

"Well na', maybe Miss Mia can tell me herself. I sees troubles in her eyes." Mia watched Auntie Cecilia pour boiling water into a large, open pot that held dried twigs and leaves.

Mia took a deep breath. She felt fuzzy in her head. "Well, my mom has a rare form of leukemia, a disease of the blood. She's getting treatments to kill off the bad blood. But after she gets them, she gets even sicker. Can you help me? Can you make a tea to make her well again?"

"Well, Miss Mia, na', that be some tall order." Auntie Cecilia placed a crackled earthenware teapot on the table next to her. From a cupboard against the wall she fetched three teacups with saucers and set them down in a row. She gave the tea a stir with a wooden spoon and then reached for a large metal strainer that hung on the wall. She started to hum softly to herself. Mia felt time was wasting. Auntie Cecilia placed the strainer over the opening of the teapot and poured the steaming brew through it into the pot.

"Well na, Miss Mia and Miss Neisha, you will be feelin' betta' when you be havin' some of my tea."

"Auntie Cecilia, what plants did you use to make this tea?" Mia couldn't help feeling curious about what ingredients were in the tea.

"Well na', that be Auntie Cecilia's secret. But don't you worry none, I would never give you anythin' that was not as good as the Lord's Gospel. This be tea from God's great gar-

"Well na, Miss Mia and Miss Neisha, you will be feelin'
betta' when you be havin' some of my tea."

dens." Auntie Cecilia looked upward then at Mia and Neisha, her eyes shining bright.

Mia took the teacup and saucer in her hand and sipped it. She stifled a grimace; it was bitter. She wondered where the sugar bowl was hiding; she needed a good dose of it to help wash the tea down. "Is this the tea that would help my mom?"

"No chile, this be an everyday kinda tea for when folks come a vistin."

"While I be makin' the tea I be thinkin' 'bout your mama. Sure nuff' I makes a tea that gets rid of the bad blood. It will give much strength to your mama during her bad times. This tea be special, it comes from de bush." Then Auntie Cecilia's face looked stern and she said, "But you must be wise and not go round picking things you don't know, for some plants are poison and they will make you ill, some can kill you dead." The air in the room was still. No one spoke. Mia looked at Neisha and saw her eyes were as wide as the saucers under their teacups.

"This here be an ancient medicine that has been passed down from our ancestors in Africa. They come on the slave ships and they be bringing with 'em all their knowledge. It take many, many year to learn all de plant's special qualities. I learn from my mama and she learn from her mama. They pass down the knowledge, that's why we be called wise women."

Mia and Neisha were silent. Auntie Cecilia disappeared behind a curtain into another room. Mia could hear her humming as she worked.

Shortly, she returned through the curtain with a burlap bag filled to the brim with a sweet smelling mixture of dried leaves and what smelled like cinnamon spice. She tied a cord around the top to keep the contents from spilling out. Then she placed it in another bag that was coated in plastic.

"This be the tea for your mama. It is made from the bark of a tree, de Keoza tree. I added some of de comfort herbs too, lemon grass and mint, so de tea smells good and the taste not be too bitta'. And lastly I be sprinklin' a pinch of de flower we here call sailor's cap! You bring this to your mama and she boil the water hot, hot. She put three heaping spoonfuls in a pot and pour de boilin' water on de top. Let it soak for a good long while, de longa' de betta'. Den she take her a strainer and pour the water through it catching up de bark an de leaves. If she like her tea sweet, honey from de bee is good. Then she drink it down three times a day til' she be feelin' stronger."

Mia reached into her bag to locate her wad of bills. She worried that she did not have enough money to pay for this huge bag of tea. She pulled out the crumpled bills, offering them to Auntie Cecilia.

"Na', na'. You jus' go and hep your mama. She be needin' you, like you be needin' her. You go na'. This here tea be a gift from Auntie Cecilia." She placed the sack in Mia's hands.

Mia blinked back tears. "Thank you! Thanks so much!"

Then, holding tight onto the sack, Mia nodded to Neisha that it was time to go.

Neisha reached out, took Auntie Cecilia's hand in her own, and said, "Thank you, Auntie Cecilia. Thank you for helpin' Mia's mama."

"You is welcome! You is welcome! You girls come back and visit old Auntie Cecilia on Peppa' Cay!"

Mia and Neisha waved their last goodbye. Once out of the gate, they jogged back to the dock without a word. They arrived to find Jack up to his elbows in conch slime. A fisherman with a large straw hat was working with him. Both Jack and the fisherman looked up as the girls approached the dock.

"You guys took long enough!"

"Jack! Look! We got the tea!" Mia cried out triumphantly.

"Great! Now get in the boat cuz we gotta get going. My friend, Mister Sanders, he is a great fisherman, and he says there may be some squalls blowing in late this afternoon. And it's gettin' to be late afternoon!"

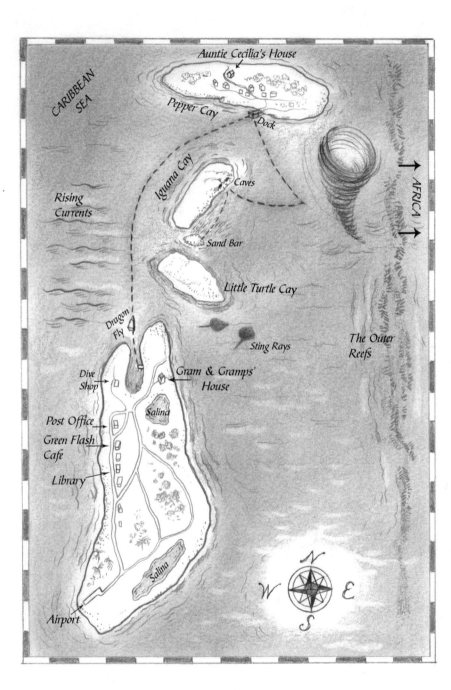

CARIBBEAN SEA

Auntie Cecilia's House

Pepper Cay

Dock

Iguana Cay

Caves

AFRICA

Rising Currents

Sand Bar

Little Turtle Cay

The Outer Reefs

Sting Rays

Dragon Fly

Dive Shop

Gram & Gramps' House

Post Office

Salina

Green Flash Cafe

Library

Salina

Airport

N
W   E
S

BLACK ROPES AND
BERRY TOES
Chapter 12

T he *Dragonfly* was cruising along, keeping clear of the reefs. Mia was enjoying the invigorating sea air. She clutched the sack of tea close to herself. Now things would change. She could go back home. She would give her mother the tea, and it would make her better. Then everything could be the way it was before. She felt exhilarated, like when she and Sam had climbed to the summit of Mt. Washington.

"Hey guys, look over there!" A rainbow arched, in brilliant hues, down to the sea. Mia exclaimed, "A rainbow! Good omen!"

Jack let out a whoop and Mia and Neisha slapped their hands together in a high five. "We've got our pot of gold." Mia held up the tea like a trophy.

The sun slipped behind a cloud. Without it, Mia felt a sudden chill. Neisha rubbed her arms. The gentle, rolling turquoise waves now had a dark cast to them.

"Hey, Mia! Where did that sun go? I got them, what you call 'em? Goose bumps?" Neisha shivered as she spoke.

"Here's a towel. Wrap it around yourself, " Mia said as she handed her one of the beach towels she had packed for the trip. Feeling the boat swaying under her feet, she looked down. "Hey, Jack, the waves are getting a little choppy, let's circle around them."

She'd hardly gotten the words out when she was pitched toward the prow of the boat. She reached to grab the side railing with her free hand, desperately clasping onto the bag of tea with the other. The water rolled and swelled beneath the *Dragonfly*, lifting it up in the air as if it were riding on the back of a giant sea monster. Then, without any warning, it slipped out from under them, slamming them back down into the sea. Neisha was rammed full force into the railing. With a terrified look at Mia, she grasped the railing with both hands and held on fast. Jack kept his station at the wheel.

"Probably just a little squall out there," Mia yelled, more to comfort herself than Neisha. She glanced in the direction the rainbow had been. It was gone, replaced by dark clouds. From the clouds poured a curtain of torrential rain, washing across the distant sea. The very sea they would have to cross to reach Bambarra.

The waves surrounding them grew stronger, lashing against the side of the boat and spraying them with salt water. Jack, his hands riveted to the wheel, kept the *Dragonfly* on course. Mia watched him with a surge of pride. As soon as they got back to Bambarra, she promised herself, she would compliment him on what a great sailor he was.

Mia was jolted out of her thoughts. There, in the sky, a short distance ahead of them, a long, black, twisting rope had emerged from the growing mass of rain clouds. It seemed to have a life of its own, pitching and snaking downward like a Kansas tornado.

Black Ropes and Berry Toes

Neisha saw the black rope and let out a high-pitched wail.

The wind slapped them with such force that Mia and Neisha both found themselves grasping on to each other with the bag of tea pillowed between them. A blast of rain struck with a vengeance. Sheets of icy needles pelted them mercilessly, leaving them drenched to the skin.

Mia felt real fear.

Neisha groaned. Mia tried to hold back rolling waves of seasickness as the boat rose up once more then smashed back down into the churning sea. Mia looked at Jack, whose face had turned a ghostly white. His glasses were askew on his face; his blue eyes shone like steel. She knew he was using every ounce of muscle in his slender body to keep the *Dragonfly* under control.

"Mia! Grab the wheel!" Jack's words rang in her ears. She danced tipsily forward, but just then the boat got hammered with yet another wave. Shaking, she pinched the bag of tea between her knees and grabbed the wheel.

"I got it!" she hollered.

"Don't let go, no matter what!" Jack's words slapped back into his face as the wind and rain tore at him. "We are heading straight into it! I gotta turn her around!"

"Okay!" Mia screamed.

Jack grabbed onto the throttle and rammed it into reverse. The boat groaned. Mia held her breath; she was terrified the boat might crack right down the middle. Instead, it lurched backward and up like a bucking bronco. Neisha hit the floor on all fours. Mia's body smashed sideways, hitting the side of the boat. WHAM! Jack had them in full gear, lunging backwards from the waterspout. The threesome watched the coiling monster in the sea in horror as the *Dragonfly* began her slow retreat.

"I'm going to punch her back into drive!" Jack warned. "Mia! Pull the wheel hard to the right. Now, Mia! Hard as you can!"

Mia obeyed Jack's commands, pulling the wheel hard to the right. The boat careened, tipping dangerously to one side. Jack's body hit her full force, pinning her to the wheel. Mia screamed and clutched her wrist, as a knifelike pain shot up her arm.

Jack took over the wheel. Mia picked up the bag of tea that had rolled out onto the floor and sank into the seat next to him. Jack drove the boat directly into the waves, cutting them in half, keeping the *Dragonfly* on a steady keel. They were making headway, with the black rope and its wrath getting farther and farther behind them.

Mia found Neisha curled up on the floor with her arms wrapped tightly around her knees and her head tucked between them. Mia sat on the floor next to her. She put her good hand on Neisha's back and gave her a brisk rub. "Breathe slow and steady; take nice, long breaths, and soon you'll get your sea legs back."

"Hey guys, we're close to Iguana Cay, we should land there and take a break. We can try again later when it settles down. What d'ya think?" Jack asked, looking at Mia.

"Okay!" Land sounded good to Mia.

Jack drove the boat close up to the shore. It was a shallow beach. He turned off the motor, raised the propeller, and easily pulled the Dragonfly onto land.

Black Ropes and Berry Toes

It was still raining. Mia and Neisha slid over the prow of the boat. Jack tied the boat to the stump of a casuarina tree as the girls searched for a dry spot. Neisha pointed to a cave nearby, and the three ran to its shelter. They found some comfortable stones for sitting and plopped themselves down, exhausted. It was dark inside the cave, and it took a few minutes for their eyes to adjust. Mia thought the place had an odd smell, like something had gone bad in the fridge. No one spoke as they sat, trying to catch their breath. Mia's wrist was throbbing. She cradled it and the tea in her other hand. She was trying to digest what had just taken place. It was surreal, like something out of a movie.

Jack was the first to recover. He started to wander off into the dark recesses of the cave. Mia fought her fatigue enough to warn him. "Be careful! Don't go too far in, you might fall into a pit. Neisha and I can't save you if you do."

"I won't get lost!" Jack's words trailed behind him; he was already out of sight.

Mia sighed. They would head back out as soon as the rain stopped. Hopefully they would make it home before nightfall.

Mia saw something move in the far corner of the cave, something that wasn't Jack. It was not a little something but a big something. It blinked beady eyes at her. She stared back in disbelief. An iguana? It had to be almost two feet long. It swished its tail as it took a step toward her. The creature cocked his head questioningly to one side. Mia didn't move. Then, as if someone had pinched him, he did a quick sprint forward, heading for Mia's red painted toes.

"Eww! Is it an iguana?" Mia asked, nearly jumping off her seat.

"Yes sir, he be an iguana! He be thinkin' your toes is sweet berries cause they is red!" Neisha giggled. "You say you want to meet an ugly old iguana, so now here he be callin' on you!"

"Yikes!" Mia tucked her toes into the floor of the cave and then stopped. "Urrgh, the sand is all wet and gooey."

"Oh no, Mia! I don't think that be sand. I think that be bat guano!" Neisha started to rise to her feet. "My Aunt Teeny, she be usin' it for fertilizer. She gets it from the caves. She got herself a prize for growin' the biggest tomato in all the islands!"

"What d'you mean bat guano? What the heck's that?" Mia was afraid she knew the answer.

"It's bat poop!" Jack said, emerging from the dark interior of the cave. "There are thousands of them in here, look above you!" Jack pointed to the top of the cave.

"Gross! Bat poop, gross! Ew, ew, ew!" Mia stood up, hopping from foot to foot. To Mia's relief the iguana scurried out of the way and hid under a rock.

Jack poked a couple of bats with a stick. Suddenly, they fluttered to life. He ducked as they swirled around his head and shoulders. With his arms flapping to protect himself, he barreled out of the cave like he was shot from a cannon. Mia and Neisha were right behind him, squealing and waving their arms to protect themselves. They fell on the white sand, laughing until their stomachs hurt and their sides were weak.

Jack, brushing himself off, called out, "The rain has slowed. Get ready for departure!" He turned his back on the girls and stomped toward the boat.

ANCHORS AWAY
Chapter 13

Mia and Neisha climbed aboard as Jack untied the boat. The sea had calmed considerably since their landing and, luckily, the tide had not shifted yet. They could see Little Turtle Cay across the channel. It would be an easy trip; they could skirt around it and avoid any close contact with the reefs. Mia inspected her wrist; it hurt when she tried to bend it.

As the boat began drifting away from the shore, Jack turned the key in the ignition. The motor rumbled and then gave out a short, raspy cough. He turned the key a second time. The motor made a long, low whine with several clicks, refusing to catch. Jack turned the key a few more times, but still, nothing happened. He waited a few more minutes.

"Maybe you flooded the engine," Mia snapped at Jack, becoming impatient. The current was gently moving them farther out along the channel between the two cays. If un-checked, it would take them out to the dangerous reef, and then to the wide-open ocean.

Jack took the key out of the ignition and spit on it.

"Gross! Why'd you have to do that?" Mia asked.

"Gramps told me if the key don't work, spit on it. It's for good luck and we need that right now!" Jack put the key back in the ignition and gave it one more turn. "If it's dead, so are we!"

"Forget the engine for a minute! Where's the anchor? We've got to throw the anchor in before we're swept out to the reef!" Mia felt a surge of panic.

Jack pulled the cushions off of a seat in the front of the boat and dug out a large silver object with sharp, pointy ends. It was so heavy he could scarcely haul it by himself. Neisha came to his aid, and the two of them managed to drag it to the aft of the boat, its rope trailing behind.

"On the count of three!" Mia shouted, "One, two, three..." The anchor hit the water with a splash and vanished. "That should hold us till we figure out what's wrong with the motor."

"Oh no!" Jack cried. "The rope! Quick, quick! Grab the rope!"

Jack threw himself at the end of the rope as it disappeared over the side of the boat. "Oh, great, it's gone!" Mia hollered at him, "Why didn't you tie it to the boat before you threw it overboard?"

"I never thought it wouldn't be tied down somewhere! Gramps never used it. We always pulled the boat ashore or tied up at a dock."

Mia looked at the water. "Well, either that was a really short rope or we are moving really fast!"

Neisha looked as if she had just eaten something that disagreed with her stomach.

"Well, this is just the pits! Grab the oars before we get swept out to the reefs!" Mia ordered.

Mia and Neisha located the paddles and each took a side of the boat. Jack stayed at the wheel and tried to steer. He gave the key one more turn, only to hear a metallic click. Mia jammed the paddle into the water and rowed with her adrenaline racing. Each stroke caused a shooting pain in her wrist. Neisha was fighting her own battle with the paddle and the sea. It didn't take Mia long to figure out that the pull of the current along with the weight of the boat was far more than they could control.

"It's not working! We're washing out toward the reef. We'll be shaved to pretty pieces out there!" Mia cried out.

"We gotta do something, Mia! We gotta turn the boat around somehow!" Jack's voice was high-pitched and shaky.

Mia felt desperate. If they hit the reef they would be shark bait. And if the boat managed to scrape through the reef, they would drift out to the ocean with nothing between them and Africa! She really regretted sneaking out the boat. She knew that she was the one responsible for what was happening to them. Because of her wanting the tea, and her hopes of returning home for the summer, she had placed all of their lives in danger.

BAM! The boat thudded to a dead stop. The impact threw Mia and Neisha into each other and slammed Jack into the back of the driver's seat. Mia pulled herself up and peered over the side of the boat to see what happened. To her surprise, the waters were parting around the *Dragonfly*.

"We've hit a sandbar!" Mia could see the sand through the waves below. "We're saved!"

"I hope we haven't sprung a leak!" Jack jumped into action. "I'll go check the bilge pump. It should come on if there's any water in the boat."

Jack stumbled like a drunken sailor off to the back of the boat. Mia looked at Neisha. "Are you okay? You were looking pretty scared."

"I'm okay. I'm glad we hit the sandbar. Maybe somebody will come find us. My daddy comes on Thursdays; maybe he be comin' for us now."

"Well, Neisha, that would be great, but we have no two-way radio in the boat, there's no cell phone service, and he doesn't have a clue where we are. We'll have to fend for ourselves."

"What you mean fend for ourselves? We can't do nothin' out here. We got to sit still and pray that my daddy comes."

"No leaks that I can find." Mia noticed that Jack's glasses were perched precariously on the end of his nose. "The pump's not working," he said as he pushed his glasses back up his nose. "Not that it would do us any good. When the tide comes up, we're gonna wash out to sea." Jack had a big streak of black grease smudged across his face. He looked like a little boy playing pirates. *If only this were all make believe*, Mia wished.

"Okay, you guys, here's the plan." Jack and Neisha stared blankly at Mia. "Everyone get a life jacket on. We have to abandon ship!"

Jack cracked his knuckles on both hands. "I can't leave the ship. I'm the Captain. Beside we can't just leave Gramps's boat. He'll be really sore if we lose it! Maybe we could pull it to shore?"

"We can't drag it the whole way to shore, that is just plain crazy. The tide would suck it right out of our hands. Besides, this boat is seriously stuck!"

"But Mia, we have to try to save the boat!" Jack pleaded.

"It is too far and too dangerous once the tide rises. Remember the boat has no motor and no anchor!" Mia continued, "My guess is that we are only about fifty yards or so off shore, all of which, I believe, is most likely to be shallow water. If we hold on to each other in a life chain, we can make it safely back to Iguana Cay."

Neisha's eyes narrowed. "No way I'm leavin' this boat. You go, but I ain't leavin'! There be stingrays out there and sharks. They be eatin' us for supper. No, ma'am, I am waitin' right here for my daddy." Neisha folded her arms stubbornly, turning her face away from Mia and Jack.

"Don't you see that when the tide comes up we'll wash out to the reef?" Mia felt like shaking Neisha. How could she not understand this?

Neisha didn't answer her.

"Neisha, this is crazy. We'll die if we stay here much longer! You have to understand about the tides!"

Neisha turned her head slowly toward Mia. Even though there was a cool breeze, her forehead glistened with perspiration. She closed her eyes and whispered, "I can't swim."

SWIMMING LESSONS
Chapter 14

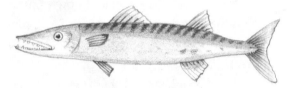

You can't swim? Your dad is a fisherman! You live on an island! How can you not know how to swim?" The words flew out of Mia's mouth like bullets.

"I never learned. My mama never taught me 'cause she never learned herself. We got no fancy pools here with life-guards and swimmin' lessons," Neisha explained defensively. "My daddy, he take the boys out in his boat to teach them to fish. I ain't never been in it."

Mia placed her hands on Neisha's shoulders and said, "No problem. It's shallow enough to walk and if it gets deep, we will keep you afloat in your life jacket. So put your life jacket on!"

Neisha shook her head defiantly. Mia held out the life jacket, but Neisha folded her arms tight across her chest.

"You and Jack go. It be best I stay here."

"No way. You can't stay. Now put on the jacket or I'll put it on you."

"You're not puttin' no jacket on me!"

"Then put it on yourself and stop acting like a baby."

"I ain't no baby. I just don't want to drown and get eaten by fishes."

"Put it on!"

"Okay, bossy lady. But I ain't leavin' this boat."

Neisha took the jacket and slowly put one arm in and then the other, but she stopped short of snapping the belts.

"C'mon Neisha, snap the belts up and I'll show you how to do a life chain out in the water."

"Can't you hear, girl? I ain't goin' in the water!"

"Snap the belts!" Mia ordered.

"Hey, Neisha, it's okay. Don't be afraid; the water isn't that deep. Mia and I will put you in the middle," Jack said, reassuringly.

"Look, Neisha, you grew up around these waters, you *gotta* know how strong the tides get! We are in a channel between two islands, and this channel does nothing but wash out to sea, but first it hits the reef and that's where the hammerhead sharks and tiger sharks live! Now, Neisha, snap it up!"

Neisha glared at Mia, then slowly snapped the vest.

"Good! Now, come with us," Mia said testily.

"Yes, I'll come. What can I do? I'm scared to drown, but I guess I'd be even more scared floating all alone in the boat with all them sharks out there. Okay, you show me what this life chain is you been talkin' about."

Mia slipped over the side of the boat, the water just above her waist. Jack waited for Neisha to climb out before climbing out himself. Mia, afraid to lose Neisha, gave directions rapid fire. Neisha was to stand in the middle between her and Jack. Mia and Jack grabbed each other's wrists behind Neisha's back.

Mia winced. "Jack you gotta hold higher on my arm, 'cause I think I sprained my wrist on the boat." Then Mia instructed Neisha to cross her arms, taking Jack's wrist in her hand, and

Jack to do the same, holding onto Neisha's wrist with a tight grasp. Neisha did as Mia directed, and with her arms criss-crossed in front of her, she clasped her hands tightly around Mia and Jack's wrists. They were now intertwined, making a chain of three. "This way we are all holding on to each other. If one link breaks we'll still have hold of each other."

"Oh, Mia, I be scared. What if a big wave come and wash us away? What we gonna do then?" Neisha asked.

"If a wave comes, you hold your breath and bob back to the surface. Remember, you can't sink with your life jacket on. Hang on to Jack and me. We'll be holding on to you."

"You sure this is gonna work?" Neisha asked nervously.

"Yes. I learned how to do it last summer. I had to go the whole width of an Olympic-size pool before I could pass my advanced swimming test."

"Ya, that be fine. But you don't have no big ocean waves or fishes in a pool!"

"Mia, I think we gotta go now!" Jack said. "The tide will turn against us soon!"

"Okay, everyone in position. Walk in a straight line and try to take our steps together like soldiers." Jack had a hold on Mia's wrist like a vise. Mia didn't want Jack to know how much her wrist hurt; she was afraid that she would be the weak link and break the chain. She had to be brave and bear the pain, no matter how much it hurt. She had to get them to shore!

The first several yards went along fine. The water stayed shallow, making it easy walking. They were able to skirt around most of the turtle grass and keep a clear footing. Then Mia saw the vast expanse of darkness ahead of them. It had to be a mile-long patch of turtle grass. If they went all the way

"You sure this is gonna work?" Neisha asked nervously.

around it, it would take twice as long to reach the shore. With her wrist throbbing under Jack's grip, she decided they would go straight through.

"Okay guys, we're going straight through the turtle grass. We'll be on shore in no time!" Mia tried to sound upbeat.

Neisha dug her feet into the sand. "No, ma'am! They be fishes in there. You can't see 'em 'cause they hidin' in the grasses."

"Neisha, do you see how far the turtle grass goes? It's just about the whole length of the beach. It would take us forever to walk all the way around it."

"No! No! There be lots of little fishes hidin' in there and the big ones come to eat 'em. I saw 'em in the turtle grasses in Bambarra. On the shore, where the pelicans be divin' for their supper, I see a shark there one day. He had him a big fin on his back and he was fishin' up a storm."

"Right! They're fishing for fish, not for us!" Mia and Jack forged ahead, sweeping Neisha along with them. Mia grimaced as the pain shot up her arm from the extra weight of Neisha's resistance. The waving blades of grass tickled her feet. She felt like she was stepping on sponges.

"This is cool. I wonder if we'll scare up a slimy old octopus."

"Thanks Jack! That's just what we want to hear right now. Don't worry Neisha, octopuses live way out in the deep water." But as Mia spoke she saw a dark shadow floating alongside her. It was long and silvery blue. It wasn't a shark. It had no fin on its back. It was a fish, just a fishy fish, nothing scary. *All will be fine, she comforted herself, as soon as we get through the grass.*

"Okay, guys, we're doing great. We'll be out of the grass soon." Mia looked over at Jack, who didn't seem to be at all unnerved by the swaying grasses. What a trooper he was. Then Mia inhaled and held her breath . . . a shadow appeared on the right side of Jack. Luckily, he seemed unaware of his traveling companion. Now they had two fish escorting them. Mia gulped. Both fish had large, ugly teeth that jutted out beyond their mouths. She prayed, *oh please, pretty please, don't let Neisha see the fish!*

The fish kept an even pace, staying unnoticed to the rear. Mia kept turning to keep an eye on them, watching that they made no sudden darts or dashes. It was odd. Mia felt she had seen this fish somewhere before, but she couldn't remember just where right now.

"Keep your eyes on shore, you guys! We're coming out of the grass! About ten more yards to land!" Mia felt a surge of relief.

Suddenly, seemingly out of nowhere, a rogue wave hit them from behind, knocking them flat as pancakes. All three were submerged, the water washing over them and the undertow sucking them backwards from the shore. Neisha let go and started flailing. In her frenzy, she hit Jack in the head and he let go of Mia's wrist. The chain was broken. Mia was the first to bob up, followed by Jack. "Shoot! I lost my glasses!" Jack called to Mia before diving back under the water.

Mia couldn't worry about Jack's glasses; she was searching frantically for Neisha's bright orange life jacket. The wave had churned the water up so much that Mia couldn't see a thing. It took all her strength just to stand upright. The salt water stung her eyes, and she blinked to focus them and gain her bearings. Then Neisha popped up, buoyant in her orange vest, coughing and spitting out salt water.

"Wow! That was a close one! Get back into the chain quickly and we'll run for shore." Mia looked out to the channel to check if any more big waves were coming. "All's clear, lets go!" The two fish were still with them, flanking them. Then it came to her in a flash: that fish looked like the one that Mom caught on vacation in Florida.

The three hit the shore and threw their bodies onto the sand. Mia scooped up the soft white grains in her hands and rubbed them all over her face. Neisha lay on her side, hugging herself. Her body was racked with spasms of coughs and shivers. Jack lay flat on his back, holding his belly; then he rolled over and threw up.

COCONUTS AND BANANA LEAVES
Chapter 15

Neisha and Jack lay prone on the sand while Mia raised herself up on one arm to search the horizon. Little Turtle Cay was in sight directly across the channel. There was not a trace of Bambarra, but Mia knew it was there, just beyond Little Turtle. She looked across the beach and up to the ridge to where the caves were; the very caves in which they had sought shelter only an hour ago. It seemed like forever.

Mia sighed deeply. She couldn't believe they were castaways. Gramps's boat was still out there in the sea, lodged on the sandbar. She was tormented by her thoughts, and she wondered if anyone would ever find them. Had she made the right decision to abandon the boat? Would Gramps's boat hold on to the sandbar and prove her wrong, or would it wash away like she predicted it would? The thought of losing the *Dragonfly* made her nauseous. Could her grandfather ever forgive her? Why had she ever carried through with this hairbrained scheme? Her grandparents would be furious with her. And when she and Jack didn't return home from "the library" they would be worried sick and call her mom. That was the last thing she wanted, to upset her mom. All she wanted was to get the tea… Then a painful realization jolted through Mia like an electric shock. Oh no! Not only had she left the boat, she'd left the tea too! In the confusion of getting Neisha out of the boat she had forgotten the tea! Hot tears streamed down her face. She lifted her hand to wipe them away, and saw that her wrist was twice its normal size and had turned a deep shade of crimson and purple.

Mia heard rustling leaves. A large green iguana poked his head out from underneath some nearby beach morning glories. It took several bold steps toward her. A smaller one scampered out of its hiding place and then froze in its tracks. Then, *pop*, out scurried another one and then another; soon there was a parade of iguanas marching down the beach toward the castaways.

"Look! Here comes our welcoming committee!" Mia roused Jack and Neisha. "There must be a dozen of them. What do you think they want?"

"Yes, they be wanting food. You betta' hide your red toes!" Neisha said as she pulled herself up into a sitting position. She waved her hand at them. "Shoo, go away, you ugly lizards!"

"Don't shoo them away. I want one." Jack said eagerly. "They'd make me a great pet. I could put one on a leash and walk it around town. How about that big guy over there? He looks like the leader of the pack." Jack stretched his arms out and advanced slowly toward the biggest iguana. "I'll name him Little Monster! Come here Little Monster, come here."

"No, sir, don't be touchin' them. They's protected by the government. That's why they is on this island. No one here to hurt them. No cats, no dogs, and no peoples, ceptin' us." Neisha rubbed her arms, trying to stop her teeth from chattering. "Ignore them and they be goin' away. What we be needin' is for us to find somethin' to drink. We left our water on the boat."

"The only water I see is salty." Mia felt the sting of real thirst.

She lay back down on the sand and closed her eyes. The sun was warm against her salt-crusted skin. She felt a sudden drowsiness overcome her. She needed to rest both her mind and body for a short while. A sleepy sort of faraway feeling settled over her. But she couldn't sleep because her head ached, and when she tried to swallow, her throat felt scratchy and sore. She stretched herself out on the beach and was immediately reminded of her swollen wrist.

Jack and Neisha stood up and wandered off toward a stand of coconut trees. Mia didn't move. She rolled over on her stomach and let herself sob. Her tears mixed with the salt and the sand. After she had a good cry, she roused herself, shaking off the sand and wiping her eyes as best she could with her good hand. She heard Jack and Neisha in the distance and decided to follow their footsteps. Mia sauntered slowly toward the stand of coconut trees. Jack and Neisha were so busy talking they didn't respond when she approached.

"Look up top. Coconuts!" Neisha wrapped herself around the trunk and used her knees to push herself up. Jack chose another tree and mimicked her. He scooted up a couple of feet and then slid back to the ground. Neisha laughed from the top of the tree as she heaved green coconuts down at him. Mia watched as they gathered up their harvest.

Neisha slid down the tree and spoke only to Jack. "I been watchin' the boys steal coconuts from people's trees; they open them up jus' like this." Neisha took the coconut in her hand, and with one strong thwack against the stone face of the cliff it cracked wide open.

Soon all three were taking turns sucking out the sweet gelatinous liquid. It was deliciously cool on Mia's parched throat. "I thought coconuts were white inside. How come this is clear and gooey?" Jack asked.

"That's cause this be a green coconut. The ones in the stores stay on the tree till they be brown and fall off. That be when the meat and the milk turn white and the shell is all hairy like a dead mans skull!"

Jack grinned. "Neisha, you're so cool. You're not like those stupid girls back home."

"Thanks, Jack, you be cool too." Neisha flashed him a quick smile. "But we ain't done shoppin' in the bush. We got us more to do."

Mia felt a surge of jealousy. Neisha was being friendlier to Jack than to her. They hardly even noticed that she had joined them. It made her angry that they acted like they were enjoying the adventure while she was left suffering with a swollen wrist and carrying all the worries. Were they thinking about the fact that they may be stuck on a desert island? Overnight? She knew she would have to be the one to come up with a plan to get them back home.

"Hey, check out these huge leaves. They are as big as an umbrella." Jack tugged at one of the bottom-most leaves.

"They's banana leaves! They be good for keepin' the hot sun away. And when the sun goes down, we be wrappin' them round us to keep us warm."

"Cool beans!" Jack started disassembling a banana tree leaf by leaf. "How many do we need?"

"We can use enough of them to make a mat to lie down on. But we don't be needin' to make a house out of them," Neisha teased. "Now we get us some aloe, for the burnt skin. "

"Aloha?" Jack asked. He tucked a banana leaf in his belt and did an imitation of a hula.

"No, not aloha. Aloe. It be a plant that grows jus' like a weed. There's a jelly inside that's good for the burnt skin. It be takin' all the pain away."

Feeling left out and wanting to be a part of things, Mia asked, "How do you know so much about plants and stuff?" Then, she added, "Neisha, I bet you could be a wise woman!"

Neisha smiled at Mia, "Here near the beach we find us some aloe. Come, snap off the tops and then rub it on your skin."

Jack followed the two girls back down toward the beach. Neisha gave him a piece of aloe. Jack smeared it all over his sunburned face. Then, grinning, he said, "See ya later, I'm going to explore the island."

Neisha and Mia took turns slathering the aloe on each other's backs and shoulders. The aloe felt cool on Mia's skin and incredibly soothing. Neisha sang softly as Mia rubbed the aloe on her.

The sun was starting to sink in the sky. They headed in the direction of the caves. On their way they found Jack hopelessly wrestling with a large tarp. He was dragging it behind him, managing to get it tangled and twisted in the bramble that he was pulling it through. Mia and Neisha ran to help.

"Look what I found! Who would have left it here?"

"That belonging to the wildlife people who come to study the iguanas." Neisha answered.

"Good job, Jack!" Mia meant the compliment. The tarp would shelter them in the likely event that they would spend the night. She had no intention of sharing a cave with bats and iguanas, not to mention bat guano! They each took an end of the tarp and dragged it down to the beach.

"Jack, do you remember the fish in our family room that Mom caught on our trip to Florida? She was so proud of it she had it stuffed and hung it on the wall."

"Yeah! That nasty barracuda."

Mia gulped, "Barracuda? Are you sure it was a barracuda?"

"Yeah, it was a barracuda, alright. The big scary guy with his ugly teeth sticking out, he could take a big bite out a' somebody." Jack made a fish face. "Why'd you wanna know?"

"Never mind, it's not important. What's important is getting this tarp up before the mosquitoes eat us alive, not to mention these sand fleas that are attacking my ankles! Then we've got to put our heads together and figure out a plan how to get out of here."

"I think we be stayin' right here! There's no needin' any more plans. We sit and wait till they come find us." Neisha crossed her arms and sat down on the tarp.

"Hold on! What do castaways do anyways? Don't they send smoke signals or raise a flag or something. We could build a giant bonfire with driftwood!" Jack suggested enthusiastically.

"Well, smart one, we don't have any matches. Maybe Neisha can find us some flints to rub together..." Mia stopped short. "Wait a minute! There's an emergency kit on the boat. Gram got it when I hurt my foot. I remember seeing some flares. If we send the flares up just after dusk, we have a chance that someone will see it and rescue us!"

"Great idea, Mia, but the flares are on the boat and we're not!" Jack gave her a disgusted look.

"I'll go." Mia noted that the boat was still on the sandbar; it hadn't reached high tide yet. "I can go fast by myself."

"NO! If you go out there again, you sure be a fool girl!" Neisha's eyes were pleading. "You must not go!"

"Yeah, Mia, you'd be crazy to go out there again. You can see from the shoreline that the tide is going out."

"Let me try. If the water's too strong, I promise I'll come right back." Mia pulled on her wet lifejacket. She rubbed her wrist. The pain wasn't going to go away, but at least she wouldn't have to do the life chain again; that had really hurt. Mia had a double motivation that pushed her forward. Not only could she bring back the flares, but she could also retrieve the tea. She gave them both a quick hug and stepped into the water. It felt cool. She strode out as far as the turtle grass. She could feel the pull of the water sucking at her feet and legs. It was much stronger than it had been earlier. She fought back her fears and took one step further. The turtle grass was slimier than she remembered. Suddenly, she slipped. She caught herself with her good hand, keeping her head above the water. She stood up, working hard to regain her balance, but the undertow was too strong to fight. She'd have to turn back.

Frustrated, Mia splashed back to shore. The whole time, her mind was spinning. *There had to be a way to get back to the boat!* She was kicking herself. If only she had thought more clearly when they left the boat. She should have remembered the tea and the emergency kit. Now they were stranded and precious time had flown by. It was all up to her; she had to do it! She had to get back to the boat!

SEA KNOTS
AND DRAGONFLIES
Chapter 16

M ia stood dripping wet on the sand. "Wow, the undertow was too strong. I had to come back."

"I told you not to go!" Jack snapped.

"You foolish girl, dat undertow can suck you down in a second." Neisha stomped her foot. "Okay! No more trips in the sea, now we work on this tarp for cover."

The threesome stretched the tarp out on the sand. It was larger than they'd thought and made of sturdy canvas.

"This is a really good tarp. Jack, did you see any poles where you found this?" Mia asked. "They had to have something to hold it up with."

"Hey Mia, look! There's a rope that goes all around the edge of the tarp." Jack's face was scrunched up as he inspected his new find. "There weren't any poles; maybe they tied it up to the palm trees." Jack untied the knot at the top end and began pulling the rope out of the hem that held it in place.

"I've got an idea, Jack. Unravel this rope. If it's long enough, we can tie it around my waist and it will give me a lifeline to get out to the boat and back."

Neisha cried, "NO! Mia, you ain't goin' nowheres! I'm not aimin' to let you get yourself drowned."

Mia found, as they freed the rope from the tarp, that there was plenty enough to reach the boat. She grabbed the end and wrapped it around her waist. "Jack, hurry, tie me one of your fancy sea knots."

"Mia, you're crazy! You *said* the undertow was too strong. I agree with Neisha. It's way too dangerous." Jack stuck his chin out.

Mia slipped the lifejacket on and handed the ends of the rope to Jack for him to tie her in tight.

"I won't tie you in so you can drown."

"Do it, little brother! Please! I gotta get the flares. And I forgot the tea on the boat."

"You're kidding! You forgot the tea?" Jack's eyes scanned the beach as if he could find it and prove Mia wrong.

"Okay, Jack and Neisha, now do you understand? I gotta get the flares and the tea!" Mia went on to explain what Jack and Neisha needed to do to secure the rope while she waded, or by now swam, back out to the boat. Jack would tie the end of the rope to his waist, giving enough slack for Neisha to wrap it around her waist too, with the very end of the rope going around a stump of the tree they had originally tied the boat up to. Mia told them to watch if she went under. They should give the line an even pull until they saw her orange life vest pop back up. She would give them a wave to let them know she was okay.

"We both think you're crazy," Jack said, nodding toward Neisha.

"I wouldn't do it if I didn't think it would work." Mia turned away from Jack. She didn't want him to see how afraid she was. Truthfully, she was scared to death. She prayed that the barracudas, or anything worse, weren't out there waiting to take a chunk out of her.

Mia took long strides into the water, making it to the turtle grass quickly. She could feel the pull of the tide as she forged on through the swaying grasses. Thankfully, the barracudas were nowhere in sight. Adrenaline pumped through her veins. She was determined to accomplish her mission. She told herself that she would make it to the boat. She would get the flares. And she would bring back the tea!

Mia found the water deeper and the waves more frequent. She dove into the waves as they rolled toward her. After each one, she surfaced and continued to doggie paddle to the boat. The sun was setting, sending a sparkling sheen across the water. She felt alone and vulnerable. She pulled on her line to make sure it was tight. When she looked to shore, she could see Neisha and Jack holding on to the end of the line. Just then, something sharp hit her leg. She panicked; all her fears about the ocean surfaced, and she screamed, taking in a mouthful of salt water. She spit it out, coughing. Her lungs were on fire. Terrified, she broke into a full swim, kicking and splashing in hopes of scaring off whatever it was that had bumped her.

Finally, Mia reached the boat and scrambled on board. She waved at Jack and saw that he was still on shore where she had left him. Neisha was staunchly holding her position. Mia quickly found the emergency kit and checked to see if she was right. Yes! It held four flares and a horn. She closed the container and stuffed it inside her life vest, snapping the belt tight. She worked as fast as she could. The boat rocked under her weight; the *Dragonfly* could break loose at any moment.

The bag of tea was sitting on the front seat of the boat. The plastic bag that covered it had kept it safe from all the rain. She secured it to her jacket with the twine Auntie Cecilia had tied it with, what felt like ages ago. Mia tied it as tightly as she could with a double knot. It was the best she could do; it was too big for her pockets, and it wouldn't fit inside her vest with the emergency kit. She wished Jack were here to tie one of his fancy knots.

Three half-empty water bottles were strewn on the floor of the boat. She stuck one in each pocket and decided she didn't have room for the third. She rinsed her mouth with the water, spitting it over the side of the boat; then, with an overpowering thirst, she swallowed the rest, leaving the empty bottle behind. She slid off the back of the boat into the water. As she moved forward, she felt the pull of the rope; Jack had already begun to haul her in. It was a comfort to know that she was attached to Jack, Neisha, and land.

The sun had set. The water was dark like ink, and she was terrified that whatever had bumped her before would come back to get her now. Mia paddled through the waves, bobbing up and down. This time, she managed to keep her head above water. She reached the turtle grass and weaved through it without a hitch. All the while she kept her eyes on Jack, Neisha, and the shore.

Suddenly, Jack began jumping up and down and yelling, "WAVE! WAVE! MIA, BEHIND YOU! LOOK OUT!" Mia looked over her shoulder. A huge wave was hurtling toward her. There was no time to think or even to panic. She reacted instinctively, making her body as rigid as a surfboard, with her arms stretched out in front of her in dive formation. She and Sam had bodysurfed so many times in the cold waters of the Atlantic Ocean that it was a natural response for her. She rode the wave, staying just on the crest of it, and let it carry her to shore.

As the wave broke on the sand, Mia landed like a beached fish. The glistening water ran off of her, making its way back to the sea. Jack reeled in the remaining rope, "Hey, surfer girl! I thought you were a goner!"

Neisha untied herself and ran to Mia's side. She threw her arms around Mia and cried, "You made it, Mia! Thank the Lord! You made it!"

"I got the flares and a horn!" Triumphantly, Mia unclipped her jacket to reveal the emergency kit. It was then she realized that only the twine was attached to her life vest. "The tea! I lost the tea! I tied it to my jacket. It must have come off when the wave hit me." Mia's eyes frantically searched the shoreline, hoping the tea would roll in on the next wave.

"Mia, look! The *Dragonfly* be movin'. She be goin' out to the sea." Neisha pointed to the receding boat.

"How am I going to face Gram and Gramps?" she wailed. Mia couldn't believe how horribly everything had turned out. She had lost the tea and Gramps's boat!

"You won't have to if we don't get the flares set off soon!" Jack said. "It's getting darker by the second. Hurry up Mia, read the directions! I can't read without my glasses!"

She wiped her tears with the back of her swollen and purple hand, and with the other hand picked up the emergency kit. In the dusky light, she began to read the instructions.

FOUR FLARES
AND A HORN
Chapter 17

Moonlight trickled through the passing clouds, allowing Neisha, Jack, and Mia to find their way through the bush. A narrow, winding trail led to the top of the ridge. Neisha veered them away from a prickly pear patch. "It be hard in this dark to see them thorns. They be stickin' long and sharp. They rip your skin open like cuttin' a ripe peach." Then she warned them not to brush against the poisonwood plant. "It be lookin' innocent, sittin' there peaceful, but it be deadly. It burns right through your skin and make you itch and swell up painful, and if you don't get treated, you could die." They climbed until they reached the top of the ridge. It was barren and covered in limestone. The mosquitoes were out in full force, buzzing in their ears.

"Why do mosquitoes always buzz in your ears?" Mia swatted her good hand over her head, slapping herself in the process.

"It'd be their music of the night," Neisha offered, dodging an insect much larger than a mosquito.

Jack examined the landscape. "I think this is the highest point. You can see in every direction. How do we set these flares off?"

"The directions say you snap it open to shoot it off. Make sure you point it away from yourself though; you don't want to lose anything important!" Then, thinking about the possibility of Jack blowing his head off, she said, "Maybe I should do it."

"No Mia, you hurt your wrist. Heck, if I can drive a boat I can set off a flare!"

"Okay, then! Snap off the top and rub the two ends together like a match on a matchbox."

Jack did as Mia said, and a brilliant burst of light shot up in the air. He held the flare for a second, then positioned it on top of a pile of rocks. It gave off the warm glow of a campfire, lighting up their faces like jack-o-lanterns. It burnt bright and steady for three minutes, then fizzled out, leaving them in darkness.

"Arggh! What was that?" Something had swooped past Mia! She covered her head with her arms.

"It be a bat coming out to eat the bugs that be eatin' us. Watch out, they like to land on your hair," Neisha warned, covering her own head with her hands.

Jack readied himself to set up the second flare. He stacked a pile of stones higher than the first pile. He snapped the top and scratched the ends together, then placed the lit flare on top of the rocks. The flare blazed, lighting up the night sky with a festive red smoke. Mia and Neisha strained their eyes toward the dark horizon. Mia thought she saw the glimmer of a light flickering. She blinked and looked again, but it must have been her imagination; no light danced upon the waters.

"We've got two flares left," Jack said, his teeth chattering from the cold and his thin frame shivering.

"Set them off, Jack! If it doesn't work soon, we'll be eaten alive." She hoped the tarp would give them some protection from the mosquitoes. Mia and Neisha were hopping from foot to foot and swatting themselves.

Jack set off the third flare. They held their breath. Then Mia saw it again, a light shimmering in the distance. "Look! There's a light. A boat is out there! Blow the horn, Jack! Blow the horn!"

Jack blasted the horn while Mia and Neisha, working together, set the fourth flare off. The girls jumped up and down, waving the flare and screaming, "Over here! We're over here!"

The light of the boat shifted position. It was turning toward them! "They saw us!" Mia yelled, "They're coming!"

Jack, Mia and Neisha ran down the ridge toward the beach. Mia's toe caught on a jagged edge of a limestone and she flew forward, landing on both of her hands. For a few seconds she saw stars, as the pain reignited by the fall shot up her arm. Jack helped her back to her feet. As she ran, she extracted small pieces of stone out of her palm.

Miraculously, they managed to avoid the prickly pear and poisonwood plants as they made their way down the path. As they caught sight of the beach, they could see that the boat was pulling up to the shore. Neisha broke into a full sprint.

"Daddy, Daddy! You came! I told 'em you'd come. I said, you just wait, my daddy will come." Neisha threw her arms around her dad's neck and he picked her up in his strong arms and hugged her tight.

"Oh, Neisha baby, thank the Lord you are all right."

As Mia approached the boat, she couldn't believe her eyes: there was Raftari sitting in the boat, watching the reunion with a huge smile on his face.

"Raftari, are we ever glad to see you!" Mia said as she waded into the water. He stretched out his hand, helping Mia climb aboard.

Jack took Raftari's hand next. "How'd you guys find us?" Raftari grinned wider, showing off his gold tooth.

"Your grands! They come for help when you be missin'. Dey say the boat be missin' too. Miss Mia, she be tawkin' bout Peppa' Cay and Auntie Cecilia. So we be goin' to Peppa' when we see de lights." He handed Jack his poncho. "You be chillin' man; dis will warm you." Jack threw it around his thin shoulders.

They sailed back home with only the headlights of the boat to guide them. Mia felt the exhaustion of the day wash over her. Her body felt like it had had hot molten lead poured over it before being blown dry with artic air. There was a high-pitched buzzing in her ears, and her head ached. She and Neisha snuggled under blankets, taking turns drinking long gulps from a jug of fresh water.

Mia wanted to rest but her mind wouldn't let her. The events of the day were haunting her like her reoccurring nightmare. Auntie Cecilia, the quest for the tea, the black rope, the sandbar, the barracuda, the undertow, Neisha not knowing how to swim, the lost tea, and, dismally, the lost *Dragonfly*!

She could hear Jack rattling on, telling his version of their adventures. He was making it all sound exciting rather than the truth, that they had all been scared to death. She wanted to sleep forever and forget everything. But she knew the or-

deal wasn't over yet; she still had to face her grandparents--
and Bianca.

Mia saw the flashlights waving as they turned into the inlet leading toward the dock. It looked as if the whole town had
shown up. They hadn't come to welcome home heroes, Mia
shuddered; they had come to see if they had made it home
alive!

The boat pulled up alongside the dock and Raftari climbed
out to tie it to the post. Mia saw Bianca first. She had her
apron all scrunched up and was wiping her eyes with it. And
then she saw Gram. She looked awful; her hair was loose and
hung limp on her shoulders, and her face, lit up by the lantern
she carried, was all red and blotchy like she had been crying. She looked old and tired. Gramps had his arm around
her, supporting her. Gramps guided Gram to the side of the
docked boat.

Mia climbed out of the boat, taking her grandfather's hand
with her good hand to steady her. Her right wrist throbbed,
but that was the least of her worries. Gramps wrapped his
arms around her and held her tight. How could she tell him
about his boat possibly being cut to pieces by the reef? How
could he forgive her?

Gramps let go of Mia and reached to help Jack out of the
boat. Mia stood frozen as her grandmother came toward her.
She was afraid of what Gram would say. But, to her utter amazement, Gram threw her arms around Mia, embracing her.

"We were so worried about you! I was so afraid something horrible had happened to you." She took Mia's face
in her hands and looked at her closely. Mia looked into her

grandmother's red-rimmed eyes. Their eyes locked and Mia felt more miserable than ever. Gram's eyes were only tired and worried; there was no trace of anger in them. Mia wished Gram would yell at her. It would be easier for her to bear than the sadness she saw.

Mia blurted out, "I lost Gramps's boat. Aren't you angry at me?"

Gram gently pushed Mia's hair away from her tear-streaked face and kissed her on the forehead. "No Mia, I am not angry with you." Mia fell into her arms and cried.

"There, there. We have time enough to talk about all that has happened later, right now all that matters is that you and Jack and your friend Neisha are home safe."

THE DAY AFTER
Chapter 18

ia woke from a deep sleep to the sound of ringing. It entered her consciousness like an electric prod. Her brain flashed back to the events of the day before. Did it all really happen? Gramps's boat? Pepper Cay? Auntie Cecilia? The lost tea?

"Mia! Phone!" Jack stuck his head in her room. "It's Mom. She wants to talk to you real bad."

"Did Gram tell her?"

"Gram called her last night and told her everything. You wouldn't know 'cause you fell asleep like you were dead!"

"Tell Mom I'll be there in a second." Mia moaned, forcing herself out of bed. She groaned inwardly. This would be the toughest of all, to hear that her mom was disappointed in her.

"Okay, but hurry!" Jack ran back to the phone.

Mia had to go to the bathroom before she could talk to her mom. She hardly recognized the blistered face that looked back at her from the mirror. Her mouth tasted like tin. She threw cold water on her face and mechanically pushed the toothbrush around her mouth with her left hand.

When she finished, she dragged herself to the phone. Only she and Jack were there.

"Hi, Mom," she said in a whisper.

"Oh, Mia, I am so *disappointed* in you!" Mia winced. "Why on earth would you think it was okay to take your grandfather's boat and go alone on some hair-brained adventure?" Mia felt a fresh wave of guilt engulf her.

"Sorry, Mom, we wanted to get this special tea." Mia's voice was raspy and her throat had an awful lump in it that made it difficult to talk. "It's supposed to cure everything... I wanted to get some for you..." Mia sniffled back a runny nose. She didn't believe in the tea anymore, now that it was gone. But she desperately needed to explain her actions to her mother. "I knew Gram and Gramps wouldn't approve of bush medicine. We just meant to borrow the boat to get to Pepper Cay. That's where Auntie Cecilia lives, on Pepper Cay, and she made us a special tea just for you. She said it was good for the bad blood."

Her mom was silent for what seemed like forever. "Mia, I know you have the best intentions, but sometimes you don't *think* the whole thing out before you act." Mia tried to hold back her tears; her mother's words hurt more than anything.

"I know. I've wrecked everything and I've lost the *Dragonfly*. All I wanted to do was make you better, so things could go back to be the way they were before, before..."

"I thought sending you and Jack away was for the best. But last night, after Gram called, I couldn't sleep from worry. All I could think about was you kids out alone in a boat in a storm. I don't know *what* Dad and I would do if anything had happened to you!"

"Oh, Mom, I miss you so much!"

The Day After

"I miss you too, honey. It's time for you and Jack to come home."

Mia couldn't believe her ears. She was going home! But, for some reason, she was not as excited about it as she had thought she would be. Was it because she had lost the tea? Now, she no longer had the hope that things would be the same as before.

Her mom did the rest of the talking, telling Mia that Dad would start making the arrangements for their flights home right away, and that she would call Gram and Gramps as soon as she knew the flight times. Mia said goodbye softly, and then placed the phone back in its cradle.

Mia had a gnawing feeling in her stomach. There was something she had to do before she could begin to think about packing her suitcase. She needed to find her grandfather. She had to talk to him alone. Mia slipped into the kitchen. Gramps was there, piling a plate high with eggs and bacon. Mia loved the smell of bacon frying and coffee brewing. She was glad to have her grandfather to herself. Empty plates were scattered on the table. Mia shoved them aside to clear an open space.

"Smells yummy, Gramps. May I join you?"

"I'm fixing this plate up for you. You must be starving! Jack ate three plates full." He smiled at her as if nothing had happened. As he placed the plate in front of her, he asked, "How is your wrist? Gram went to town to fetch the doctor."

"Um, my wrist hurts, I think it's sprained." Mia munched on a crisp piece of bacon. "I wanted to tell you how sad I am about your boat. I did a stupid thing to sneak the boat out. I'm so sorry about the *Dragonfly*. She was a beauty. How can I ever make it up to you?"

"Mia, you and Jack are more precious to me than any boat could ever be. I'm grateful that nothing catastrophic happened out there. You certainly did make some unwise decisions, such as doing the trip on the sly. But Mia, you were absolutely right about abandoning the boat. If you had stayed, all of you could have drowned. The divers went out early this morning and found the *Dragonfly*. The reef had ripped her hull wide open. She sank just past the reef."

"Gramps, I'm so sorry." Mia could no longer hold back her tears. Gramps reached over and patted her good arm.

"Mia, you put yourself, your friend, and Jack in serious danger. But you still made some very brave decisions. And now that your mom has decided to have you and Jack return home for the remainder of the summer, you have to be the bravest of all." Gramps's blue eyes met hers. Mia looked down at her swollen wrist. She didn't like what she saw in Gramps's eyes. She didn't want to hear what he was going to say. "Mia, your mother..."

Mia jumped up from the table. "Oh my gosh, I gotta take a shower before the doctor gets here." She charged out of the kitchen, seeking the refuge of her bathroom.

Mia did the best she could to splash water on herself. She squirted shampoo on her head and then let the water rinse it out, but it was really hard to do with only one hand. She toweled off and, still half wet, began the exhausting job of dressing herself. By the time she had finished, the doctor had arrived and Jack was quick to let her know.

"Well, young lady, you did quite a good job of banging up your wrist. It looks like a very bad sprain, along with what I believe is a compound fracture. I'm going to have to set it in a cast up to your elbow." The doctor set to work and finished by tying her arm in a sling. "There, that should hold you for about six weeks. When you get home you can have your doctor check it. You won't be able to get it wet, so no swimming for the rest of the summer. When you shower you will have to have a plastic bag on your arm so no water seeps in. I will leave some salve for your sunburn. Drink lots of liquids and stay out of the sun!"

Mia mumbled a feeble thanks to the doctor and shuffled over to the hammock. She stood there staring at it: she realized that if she could somehow manage to plop herself into it, she would never be able to climb back out, at least not without help. *Oh what a mess*, she thought. *I won't be able to help mom with only one hand. I surely won't be able to go to camp or ride my wave board or a horse. I can't even stay here and wait tables with Neisha.* The lump in her throat came back as she swallowed hard to hold back a new gush of tears.

ISLAND FRIENDS FOREVER
Chapter 19

M ia felt glum as she climbed out of the back of the pickup truck. She and Jack were going with Gram and Gramps for a goodbye dinner at The Green Flash Café. She was surprised when Gram had suggested it, saying it would be fun to eat out their last night on the island. But now that she was going home, she felt a deep sadness. She didn't want to say goodbye to her island friends.

"Wow, the place is lit up like a Christmas tree!" Jack exclaimed. He was right. The outside of the café was decorated with dozens of lights and paper lanterns. Mia stepped through the door and blinked in amazement. The Green Flash was bustling with customers! Twinkling lights were hung all along the rafters and red and pink Chinese lanterns dangled from the beams and fluttered in time with whirling paddles of ceiling fans. A space near the bar had been cleared for a dance floor. Huge speakers had been set up and were being tested for sound. Mia felt the beat of the conga drums and smiled in delight at a man rubbing a screwdriver along the teeth of an old hand saw, keeping perfect time. The rhythm was contagious.

Neisha sashayed across the dance floor.

"Hey Neisha! Wanna dance?" Jack placed his hand in his pockets and rocked back and forth on his cowboy boots.

"I fear for my feet if I be dancin' with you in them boots. They got points!" Neisha laughed and grabbed his arm, pulling him onto the makeshift dance floor. She wore a new pair of blue jeans and a crinkly white peasant-style blouse. She held her head high, showing off a new hairdo. It was pulled tight against her head in rows of tiny braids from her forehead to the crown of her head, and from there her hair cascaded into a mass of curls that bobbed and danced with her every movement.

Mia, not being in the mood to dance with a cast on her arm, looked across the room at Bianca. She was busy adorning each table with a big pink conch shell. Her hips swayed to the music as she tucked red and pink hibiscus blossoms into the shells' open mouths. Mia hadn't seen Bianca or Neisha since the night on the dock, which now felt like ages ago. Bianca caught her eye and smiled her warmest smile, waving a handful of cut blossoms at her. Mia breathed a sigh of relief; it sure didn't seem that Bianca was mad at her.

Neisha's daddy was there, too. He had donned a chef's apron around his ample middle and was busy lighting the grill. Lobster tails and tuna steaks were stacked up high on plates. Drops of sweat rolled down the sides of his face as he stoked the fire to near bonfire level. Platters of mango salsa, fried peas and rice, with large wooden bowls of chicken salad, coleslaw, and macaroni salad, were placed picnic style on the table in front of the grill.

Bianca breezed by, tucking a fresh blossom in Mia's curls. Then, laughing and waving at the flames, she said, "With dat big bonfire, you gonna be cookin' more than fish!" Neisha's dad chuckled and fanned the flames higher. The whole café buzzed with excitement.

Mia watched Gram and Gramps mingle from table to table. Gramps had on his Hawaiian shirt with the pink hibiscus blossoms, Mia's favorite. And Gram looked elegant in her turquoise dress and crystal necklace that sparkled against her tanned skin. They were relaxed and at ease, talking and laughing like cheerleaders at a pep rally. Mia never saw her grandmother look so at ease and so… so… *social*!

Making a grand entrance, Raftari strode into the café, sporting a magnificent floor length caftan in earthy brown tones and golden hues. His usually unruly hair was hidden beneath a matching turban.

Mia called to him, "Raftari, you look so handsome tonight! Did you bring Sandy?"

"Oh, yes, my bee-u-tiful lady. Sawndee' would not miss saying goodbye." Raftari motioned for her to join him as he sauntered to the back of the café. Mia roared with laughter when she caught sight of Sandy. Her head poked comically through the open window. On top of her head she sported a floppy straw hat with two holes cut out for her ears, each jutting out at different angles. Tied under her chin was a big yellow bow, holding her hat in place. Mia reached out and

rubbed her velvet nose. "Sandy, you're all dressed up like you're going to a party! You are too cute for words!"

"Sawndee', she has brought a goodbye present for my bee-u-tiful lady." Raftari grinned at Mia, showing off his gold tooth. Then, as if he were a magician pulling a rabbit out of a hat, he reached through the window and produced a bur-lap sack from Sandy's saddlebag. Mia stood there, speechless, staring at what Raftari held in his hands. "This be a present from Auntie Cecilia. It be the tea for your mama."

"But...how? When? Oh, my gosh! Really? Is it really the tea? You wouldn't tease me, would you?" Mia couldn't believe it was true.

"Raftari no tease! This be the true tea. Neisha's papa and me, we take us a trip on de boat, to visit Auntie Cecilia. We tell her about the storm comin' and your grand's boat hittin' de reef. She say, this be the tea that Mia does need. She say you must be bravest of all to go home to your mama. She be givin' you and your mama the tea of hope mixed with plenty, plenty, strength. She say, Mia must be brave!"

Raftari handed the sack full of tea to Mia. She clasped it with her good hand and hugged it. "How can I ever thank you? You and Auntie Cecilia? Oh, and I must thank Neisha's daddy too!" Mia's head was spinning; she couldn't believe that they had secretly made the trip to get the tea. It sure felt won-derful to have it in her hands and be able to bring it home!

Mia planted a big kiss on Raftari's cheek. "Thank you so much! I have to tell Neisha and Jack! They'll be so surprised! And Gram and Gramps!"

"Oh, my bee-u-tiful lady, your grands', dey know. Dey ask Neisha's papa to get the tea for you. So dis be a present from everybody! And Neisha, she be knowin' about de tea, she want to go wit her papa, but he say no, not till she be learnin' how to swim."

Tears rolled down Mia's cheeks. She didn't bother to wipe them away. They were happy tears.

Holding on to the tea, Mia flew across the dance floor to find her friend. She had to show Neisha the tea and thank her. She had to thank everyone!

Mia found Neisha with Jack in the throng of dancers and pulled her from the dance floor, leaving Jack to spin around by himself.

As soon as they were away from the crowd, Neisha leaned close to Mia, covered her mouth with her hand, and whispered, "I got a secret to share."

"No! No more secrets!" Mia teased.

"It be my good news," Neisha said softly.

"Good news! Okay! Tell me!"

"I be going to high school in September." Mia's eyes opened wide in surprise. Neisha's face was glowing.

"Excellent! That sure is great news! But how?"

"Remember my friend Tika? She be on the big island with her mama? They say I can live with them for school days. And my daddy says he be willin' to take me on his boat Monday mornings to the big island. But first he be teachin' me how to swim. He say no goin' on any boats till I pass the daddy swim test. And the best part is that on Friday's he be deliverin' the fish and me to my mama!"

"I'm so happy for you! That's perfect! You get to come home every weekend!"

"Yes, I won't be missing mama so much this way."

"But now, the only thing is… Well, I'm going to miss you! I don't really want to say goodbye tonight." Mia blinked back her tears.

"That be okay. I be coming back home for a long time at Christmas. You come visit me and your grands then. Now you got to go home and give your mama the tea, then maybe she be strong enough to come to Bambarra too."

"Neisha, thanks for helping get the tea. Now I can go home!" Mia threw her good arm around Neisha's neck and gave her a hug. "I'll be back! We are island friends forever!"

GLOSSARY

- **Aft** – The back of a boat.
- **Aloe** (ah-low) – A plant that has a gel inside its leaves which gives relief from the pain of sunburn.
- **Barracuda** (Bar-ra-cu-da) – A long, thin tropical fish with a protruding lower jaw that exposes fierce, fang-like teeth.
- **Bat guano** (gwa-no) – Dung of bats found in caves and harvested as a fertilizer for plants.
- **Bilge** – The lowest part of a boat.
- **Bilge pump** – A pump used to remove water from the bilge.
- **Bush** – Area of land thickly covered with various low growing plants.
- **Cay** (key) – A small island.
- **Conch** (konk) – A large sea snail that lives in a brightly colored shell. The snail is removed by cutting a hole in the top of the shell. The meat is hammered and marinated before it is cooked due to its very rubbery consistency. A true Caribbean delicacy.

- **Green Flash** – A bright flash of green light that appears the second before the sun sets on a clear ocean horizon. Sighting of the green flash is rare and thought to bring good luck to anyone who witnesses it.
- **Inboard Motor** – A motor located on the inside of a boat; the propeller is outside on the back of the boat.
- **Leukemia** (loo-key-me-a) – A disease found in bone marrow. The white blood cells are produced in large amounts, taking over the red blood cells. The person suffers from being tired, which is caused by the lack of the red blood cells.
- **Marijuana** (mar-a-wan-na) – A plant that when dried and then smoked produces a feeling of euphoria.
- **Mirage** (mi-raj) – An illusion of water caused by strong sunlight, often seen on a desert.
- **Poisonwood** – A plant found in Africa and the Caribbean. Its leaves contain a substance that when rubbed or touched to the skin causes a severe swelling and irritation.
- **Prickly Pear** – A cactus that thrives in hot, sandy regions. It grows tall and wide and has large, very sharp thorns. The fruit of this cactus is edible.
- **Prow** – The front of a boat.
- **Puddle Jumper** – A small airplane with propellers. Often used to get from one island to another.
- **Rasta man** – A person who is a member of the Rastafarian Religion. The religion originated in Jamaica, and the followers believe that Africa is the Promised Land.

- **Reef** – A ridge of coral and rock that reaches to the surface of the ocean. A reef creates a barrier between an island and the deeper ocean. Reefs have been the cause of many shipwrecks.
- **Reggae** (reg-ay [long a]) – A very popular type of Caribbean music that started in Jamaica. It is a mixture of several types of music, including soul, calypso and rock and roll.
- **Salina** (sa-li-na) – A low-lying body of water with a high quantity of salt. Water is channeled into the salina from the ocean and then allowed to dry. Salt crystals are raked from the salina and sold.
- **Stingray** – A flat, triangular ray (fish) with a long whip-like tail that contains a poisonous stinger that can cause severe injury.
- **Waterspout** – A whirlwind of tornado force that occurs over water.

REFERENCES

Defries, Amelia. *The Fortunate Islands.* London: Cecil Palmer, 49 Chandos Street, Covent Garden, WC2, 1929.

Hanna-Smith, Martha. *Bush Medicine in Bahamian Folk Tradition.* Miami: Dodd Printers, 2005.

Houghton Mifflin Co. *American Heritage Dictionary, Third Edition.* Reference for glossary definitions.

Keegan, Bill and Betsy Carlson. *"Caves."* Times of the Islands. Winter 2006/2007. (Article containing information about bat guano, cockroaches and cave crickets.)

Manco, Bryan Naqqi, Environmental Officer of The Turks and Caicos Islands. A specialist in the flora and fauna of the islands.

The Turks and Caicos National Museum. Grand Turk, Turks and Caicos Islands, BWI

Wood, Kathleen McNary. *Flowers of the Bahamas and the Turks and Caicos Islands.* Oxford, UK: Macmillan Caribbean Publishers Ltd., 2003.

Woodring, Marsha Pardee. *"Boundaries of the Possible: The Little Water Cay Rock Iguana Nature Trail Program."* Times of the Islands. Winter 1997.

Weedon, Matt and Angela Weedon. *"Islands of time."* Times of the Islands. Fall 2001. (Article about Gibbs Cay Stingrays.)

ABOUT THE AUTHOR

The love of children and children's literature has played an integral role in Donna Seim's life. In her first book, *Fifty Cents an Hour*, Donna tells her hilarious childhood stories from growing up in a large Irish Catholic family.

Donna's first picture book, *Where is Simon, Sandy?*, set in the Caribbean, is an award-winning story of a little donkey that wouldn't quit.

Hurricane Mia, a Caribbean Adventure, is Donna's first novel. And, coming soon, is *Charley!*, the story of an orphaned city boy from Boston who sings his way into a dairy farming family in the heartland of rural Maine.

When Donna is not in the Caribbean, she lives in Newbury, Massachusetts, with her husband and her dog, Rags.

Donna is a graduate of Ohio State University, and holds a master's degree in Special Education from Lesley University.

You can visit Donna at www.donnaseim.com.

Be sure to join Hurricane Mia on Facebook and follow her on Twitter @hurricanemia!

Hurricane Mia and the Green Flash Café: A fun time PARTY to chill out!

Invite your best group of friends for a fun lunch at the Green Flash Café !

Send out invitations

- Cut out conch shell shapes or palm trees out of brown paper bags.
- Use rubber stamps and magic markers to decorate.
- Give time, place and what to wear: cut-off shorts, t-shirts, and flip-flops!

The Café

- Find a porch or shady spot in your backyard.
- Set up a long folding table or several short ones to make a bar.
- Cover with bright colored fabrics.
- Decorate with Palm leaves and coconuts.
- Hang paper lanterns and twinkling lights.
- Set up café-style with small tables and chairs or stools.
- Place flowers in seashells on the tables.

- Make a Green Flash Café sign, good eats, and cold drinks!
- Play reggae music!
- Use your imagination!

Menu

- Hurricane Mia's Delight - Mix in blender: tropical Mango juice, ginger ale, and a scoop of frozen yogurt – serve in a tall glass with little umbrella.
- Fried fish fingers, fried chicken, crab cakes, French fries, coleslaw, fried rice &beans.

Desserts

- Fresh fruit cups with papaya, mango, and watermelon, drizzled with shaved coconut!

Games

Catch the Barracudas!

- Find a nice big box with an open top; glue colored paper to it.
- Make two fishing poles with cut-off dowels and string.
- Cut magnetic tape into small squares, and hot glue to the end of the string.
- Cut out barracuda shapes from cardboard.
- Throw in some surprises, like sharks and stingrays.
- Attach a metal grommet to all of the fish.
- Number each one from 1 to 24. They are worth that many points when you catch them. Sharks and stingrays are worth extra points like 25 or 30!

- Break into two teams.
- Keep score, the team with the most points wins!
- You can add to the fun by taping questions about the book on each fish. The team has to come up with the right answer to keep their points; if they miss they have to throw the fish back in!

Pin the Tail on Sandy

Just like pin the tail on the donkey!

- Use the picture of Sandy on the back cover to help you draw a large horse without a tail.
- Hang it up on a flat surface.
- Find some old rope, cut into horse tail lengths,(to match Sandy's size)
- Give each of your guests a tail and have them decorate it. They can unravel it and braid it. You can also use yarn. Add bright-colored ribbons and beads. Wrap double-sided sticky tape to the top of the tails.
- Tie a blindfold on each participant (one at a time) and spin three times.
- First touch of the tail is where it stays!
- When all the tails are on Sandy, take a picture of all your guests and Sandy with all her tails, you can email them each a picture later!
- Let your guest take home their decorated tails!

Party Favors

- Place a fortune-telling note in little muslin bags with loose tea. Make each fortune fun and upbeat, and each one different, tie with twine and hand out as party favors!

  (If you can't think of fortunes you can have each guest as they arrive write down a wish as if it were a fortune. For example, if they wish they had a horse, they would write, "you will one day have your own horse"! Mix them all up and put them in the tea bags. It will be fun to see who gets each other's wishes!)

Bonus Fun Activity

- Paint all your guests' toes with red nail polish! While toes are drying is a great time to discuss *Hurricane Mia*!

When _____
Where _____
What to wear _____

You're Invited . . . .

Photocopy and enlarge your conch invitation!

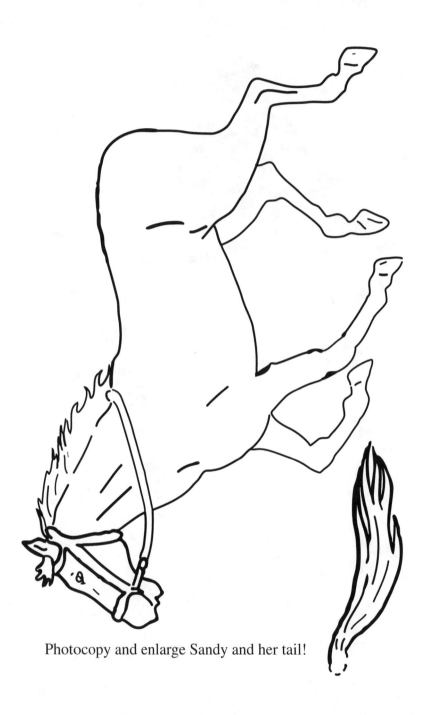

Photocopy and enlarge Sandy and her tail!

LET'S TALK ABOUT HURRICANE MIA!

Mia was sent away for the summer with her little brother. Did you ever have to go somewhere you didn't want to? Have you ever planned something fun to do with a friend only to find out it couldn't happen?

In the beginning, Mia feels alone. Have you ever felt you were all alone and that no one around you understood how you felt?

Mia and Gram don't get along. Have you ever had an adult member of your family that you didn't get along with? Why do you think Mia has so much trouble with her grandmother?

Mia and Neisha made friends fairly quickly. Have you ever made a friend when you weren't expecting to? Why do you think the two girls became such good friends?

What do Mia and Neisha have in common? How are they different?

Jack is a thorn in Mia's side. Do you have a younger brother or sister that always wants to be with you? Did your parents ever make you be with them even when you had much better things to do?

Do Mia's feelings about Jack change during the story?

Why do you think Mia is always getting into trouble? Do you think her grandmother really doesn't like her?

The tea that cures everything becomes very important to Mia. Why do you think it becomes so important to her? Do you think she risked too much for it?

Does Mia really believe that the tea will cure her mother? What do you think Mia's major motivation is in bringing the tea to her mother?

Mia lets Jack in on her plan. Why would she do that when he drives her crazy? What is going on with Jack all this time?

Neisha has a problem. The only high school is on another island. If you were Neisha how would you feel?

If you were Mia, would you go searching for an Auntie Cecilia and her tea? How did Mia feel when she first met Auntie Cecilia?

Mia makes the big decision when they hit the sandbar that they must leave the boat. Why won't Neisha come? Why does Neisha change her mind in the end?

What happens to the tea? How does Mia lose it? What does the tea symbolize to Mia?

They say it takes a village to raise a child. How did all the main characters become involved in Mia's search for the tea?

Which part of the book did you like the best? If you were to pick your favorite part to read aloud, which part would that be?

Which was your favorite character? Why? If you picked a second favorite character which one would that be?

This is really Mia's story. How would it change if Neisha told the story from her point of view? Jack? Gram?

Did you like the ending? If you were to write your own ending what would you change it or would you leave it as it is?

Also by Donna Marie Seim
and PublishingWorks, Inc.

WHERE IS SIMON, SANDY?

Set on the Caribbean island of Grand Turk, Simon, the deliverer of water, falls ill. It is up to his faithful donkey, Sandy, to fulfill his duty. Sandy's story is charmingly depicted in vibrant watercolors. Based on the true story of the intelligence and loyalty of Sandy the donkey who saved the day by delivering water to the island's inhabitants.

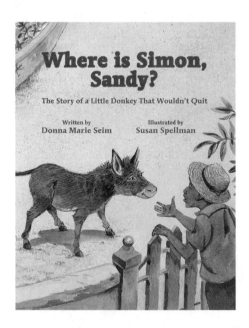